Welcome to the dark side of the galaxy . . .

Bebo pointed at the ground. "Right there! Right there! We were walking along and *poof!* she was gone!"

"Walking along, you say? Are those your footprints, then?" Chood pointed at a line of footprints in the dirt road.

"Yes! That's where I was."

"Then where are your friend's footprints?" the Enzeen asked.

"Why, they're right . . ." For the first time, Bebo stopped muttering to himself. There were no other footprints in the ground. There was no sign that anyone but Bebo had been standing there. "But she was right there! Right there!"

Chood looked very sorry for Bebo, and sorry that the others had been disturbed. He shrugged. "You see. He is quite mad. It is most regrettable."

As the others turned away, Tash said softly to Bebo, "I'm sorry I can't help you. I wish there was something I could do for you."

Bebo gave her a cold, hard look. "It doesn't matter. Before long you'll be dead. You're all going to die."

Look for a preview of Star Wars: Galaxy of Fear #2, *City of the Dead*, in the back of this book!

MIKE'S
FAMOUS BOOKSTALL
BOOKS SOLD &
EXCHANGED

STAR WARS®
GALAXY of FEAR

BOOK 1

EATEN ALIVE

JOHN WHITMAN

BANTAM BOOKS
NEW YORK · TORONTO · LONDON · SYDNEY · AUCKLAND

For my wife, Lisa, who always rescues me

EATEN ALIVE
A BANTAM BOOK : 0 553 50652 8

First publication in Great Britain

PRINTING HISTORY
Bantam edition published 1997

All rights reserved.
® TM, & © 1997 Lucasfilm Ltd

Copyright © 1997 Lucasfilm Ltd
Published originally in the United States by Bantam Doubleday Dell, Inc.

Cover art copyright © 1997 by Lucasfilm Ltd

Condition of Sale
This book is sold subject to the condition that it shall not,
by way of trade or otherwise, be lent, re-sold, hired out
or otherwise circulated without the publisher's prior consent
in any form of binding or cover other than that in which
it is published and without a similar condition including
this condition being imposed on the subsequent purchaser.

Bantam Books are published by Transworld Publishers Ltd,
61–63 Uxbridge Road, Ealing, London W5 5SA,
in Australia by Transworld Publishers (Australia) Pty Ltd,
15–25 Helles Avenue, Moorebank, NSW 2170,
and in New Zealand by Transworld Publishers (NZ) Ltd,
3 William Pickering Drive, Albany, Auckland.

Printed and bound in Great Britain by
Cox & Wyman Ltd, Reading, Berkshire.

EATEN ALIVE

PROLOGUE

The security door slid open with a hiss. A dark figure stepped into the laboratory, where a single scientist stood over an examination table. On the table, something was still alive.

As the dark figure approached, the scientist did not turn around. Only two other beings in the entire galaxy had access to his hidden fortress, and he knew who had come to see him.

"Welcome, Lord Vader," the scientist said.

The figure covered in black armor took a step closer. His face was hidden behind a black, skull-like breath mask. He was Darth Vader, Dark Lord of the Sith, the cruel right hand of the Emperor of the galaxy. "Have you completed your research?"

The scientist turned. In his hands he held a sharp, hooked instrument. Behind him, the creature on the table shuddered, then grew still.

"Very nearly. The first five stages of my experiment are under way. Soon I will be able to complete the sixth and final stage. Then I shall provide the Emperor with the greatest power in the galaxy."

"That claim has been made before," Vader said. "The Death Star was supposed to be the ultimate mechanical terror. It destroyed the planet Alderaan, but then the Rebels destroyed the Death Star."

1

"Pah!" the scientist replied. "That battle station was a toy. My designs are not machines . . . I control the power of life itself. I will create the ultimate weapon for the Emperor."

"The ultimate weapon," Vader cautioned, "is the Force."

"Of course, of course."

Vader stared at the scientist for a moment, his breath rasping through his mask like a threatening hiss. "You are running out of time. Already your work may have been discovered."

The scientist scowled. "You mean by *him*? Don't worry about *him*. I will deal with him when the time comes."

Vader raised one hand in caution. "If this secret should leak as did the secrets of the Death Star, the Emperor and I will be most displeased."

Then the Dark Lord turned away.

The scientist stared after the armored figure, his eyes burning a hole into Vader's back. Soon, he thought, very soon, he would have the power to destroy even Darth Vader. Then he would take his place at the Emperor's side.

He turned back to his experiments. He lowered his hooked blade. On the table, the creature screamed. . . .

CHAPTER

The attack came without warning.

In a small quadrant of space, an X-wing starfighter altered its flight path slightly to avoid the massive red moon looming ahead. As it did, a twin-ion engine ship, or TIE fighter, appeared in the moon's shadow, its two solar panels glinting with reflected light. Streaking through the void, the TIE opened fire, its dual turbo-lasers spitting out streaks of flame.

One of those laser shots creased the X-wing's hull. The X-wing's shields deflected most of the blast, and the shaken fighter banked away and accelerated to attack speed.

Relentlessly the TIE fighter followed. Not only was the TIE fast and maneuverable, but the pilot had an added advantage. She knew her opponent. She eyed him

3

coldly as he twisted and turned in an effort to shake off his pursuer. But she stuck with him, sparing only quick glances at her tactical display, waiting for her target to fall into her sights.

She grinned. "Yo are mine."

The fleeing X-wing made a sharp course adjustment and headed straight for the small red moon. That pilot knew who was behind him. It was the same enemy he had faced a hundred times. She was good. If he was going to survive, he would have to be better.

"Try this," he challenged.

The X-wing pilot aimed the nose of his ship at the moon. Instantly the moon's gravity grabbed hold of him, and his speed increased. At the last possible moment, the pilot veered away. Keeping just within gravity's reach, the X-wing pilot gunned his engines and scraped along the moon's atmosphere. The belly of his ship left a trail of flames in the air as the tiny ship looped around the moon.

The effect was like a slingshot. Pulled forward by gravity, the X-wing hurtled around the moon's perimeter, far ahead of the pursuing TIE fighter. He came around the farside with his own lasers firing.

But the TIE pilot was ready for him. "Oldest trick in the manual!" she gloated. She had changed her course to intercept her quarry before he completed his backdoor maneuver, blasting the X-wing with laser fire. The X-wing jerked hard left in a desperate roll. Laser bolts exploded around his ship, but amazingly, not a single shot hit him. Laughing, the X-wing pilot scooted past the TIE fighter, then curled around to continue the dogfight.

"You are so lucky," the TIE pilot snapped.

Suddenly a metallic hand as large as the red moon descended from the heavens to block the X-wing's path. But the starfighter passed right through it.

The owner of the hand looked down at the holotable where the starfighter combat had taken place. He was D-V9—or Deevee for short—a silver droid designed to imitate the appearance and behavior of humans. Since his head and face were made of durasteel, the droid couldn't frown, but it gave the definite impression of doing just that. "Tash. Zak. Stop this ridiculous game."

The two pilots dropped their control disks, and the holographic starfighters, tiny in comparison to the droid looming over them, immediately froze in place. They hung in midair over the holotable, along with the computer-generated moon and planet that served as a playing field.

The holotable was in a corner of a small lounge, which was in the forward compartment of a star cruiser called the *Lightrunner,* which was at that moment hurtling through hyperspace.

The X-wing pilot stood up from the holotable. His name was Zak Arranda. He brushed back a lock of his messy brown hair and grinned at his opponent.

The TIE fighter's pilot was his sister, Tash. At thirteen, she was a year older than her brother, and an inch taller. Her thick blond hair was arranged in a neat braid, and her lightly freckled face was turned down in a serious frown.

"You are *sooo* lucky," she repeated.

"That was prime!" Zak laughed. "And anyway it's not luck, it's skill."

Tash wasn't convinced. "No one could have gotten away from that barrage. Besides, everyone knows all hologames are rigged so the Imperial ships have an advantage. The Empire would never let anyone else come out on top. But you always win." She shook her head. "I just don't get it."

"What you will get," said the impatient droid beside her, "is dull-witted from playing hologames. They're an utter waste of time. Besides, it's time for your zoology lesson." The droid put his hands on his swivel-socketed hips and waited.

"Lessons?" Zak groaned. "We're in the middle of hyperspace!"

Deevee delivered the electronic version of a sniff. "There is no respite from learning."

Or from bionic baby-sitters, Zak thought; aloud, he argued, "But hologames *are* educational. They improve hand-eye coordination and encourage quick thinking, and—"

"And we're ready for lessons, Deevee," Tash interrupted.

Not that she was very interested in zoology. She would much rather be reading one of her data files on Jedi lore or downloading information from the HoloNet. But sometimes it was good to set an example for a younger brother.

Besides, she hated—*really* hated—being the Imperial TIE fighter—ever since the Empire had blown her and Zak's homeworld of Alderaan to bits. Zak and Tash had been away for two weeks and had returned home to find that, well, their home was gone. Their parents, friends, and neighbors were all killed in the explosion.

Deevee punched a few commands into the holotable's control panel. "Zoology lessons," the droid muttered to no one in particular. If he could have, he would have rolled his eyes. "I have the brain capacity of a supercomputer and I'm giving zoology lessons."

Zak and Tash hardly noticed. Deevee had been complaining about his new job since the day they had come to live with Uncle Hoole.

D-V9 was a class-one scientific research unit with an OmniTask computer brain fast enough to calculate and record ten million bits of information about alien cultures per second. He had been carefully designed to help his master, Hoole the anthropologist, with important research into cultures across the galaxy. He was the envy of every droid he knew—until six months ago, when he was stuck with the job of caretaker to two young orphans.

Deevee didn't like his new assignment, and he reminded Zak and Tash of it every chance he got.

At the droid's command, the star-battle program melted away and was replaced by a stream of holograms detailing various animals throughout the galaxy. The program settled on one odd image: an enormous, fanged beast, sitting without moving while three or four tiny birds fluttered in and out of its mouth. A recorded voice said: "One of the more unusual relationships in galactic nature is this one. The bloodthirsty rancor will kill everything it sees . . . except the gibbit bird, which roams freely inside the rancor's mouth. The rancor allows this because the gibbit birds pick the flesh from the rancor's jaws, and this helps keep the rancor's teeth clean. . . ."

Unfortunately, as the zoology lesson continued, Tash found herself drifting off. She was a good student, but science was not her favorite subject. Tash slipped a datapad out of her pocket and held it in her lap, where neither Zak nor Deevee could see it. She keyed in a command, and the screen lit up with lines of text.

It was a story about the Jedi Knights.

It was also illegal. Legends of the Jedi Knights had been banned by the Empire since before Tash was born. But one day Tash had come across a story uploaded onto the galaxywide communications service known as the HoloNet. Sitting at her desk in her room on Alderaan, Tash could sign on to the HoloNet and scan libraries on distant planets or talk to people on worlds light-years away. One day she discovered a coded message filed under a word Tash had never seen before: *Jedi*. It had taken her hours to break the code, but finally the file had unscrambled before her eyes.

The story Tash discovered was written by someone code-named Forceflow, and it told the history of the Jedi Knights, a group of people who used something called the Force to protect the galaxy from evil.

According to the story, the Jedi Knights had been the guardians of the Old Republic for a thousand generations. The only weapon a Jedi carried, Tash had learned, was a lightsaber, a handheld weapon made of pure energy. But the Jedi used violence only as a last resort. Instead they relied upon a mysterious power known as the Force.

Curious, Tash had sent a message to ForceFlow, hoping to learn more. But ForceFlow didn't respond, and his original story was erased from the Net.

After that, Tash kept her eye out for any information on the Jedi. She visited libraries, scanned the Net, and talked to anyone who had a story about the Jedi or knew of the Force. She hoped to meet a Jedi someday. She hoped to *be* one someday. But soon after the first story was wiped from the Net, all information about the Jedi vanished from the public records. It was replaced by a single report, stamped with the Imperial seal, stating that the Jedi had died out when the Old Republic gave way to the Empire. According to the official reports, the Jedi were . . .

"Extinct," Deevee droned. "Imagine that."

Tash looked up from her datapad. D-V9 was standing beside the image of a flock of blue-winged birds. The image was fading, and Deevee was obviously wrapping up his commentary. She had missed the entire lesson.

"Well, that's enough for today," the droid said. "There will be an exam on this lesson next week."

Excused by their tutor, Zak and Tash escaped from the lounge. Tash looked at her brother and could see that she wasn't the only one who'd been daydreaming.

"What's on your mind?" she said.

"Home. Alderaan. Skimboarding in the park." Zak paused. "Mom and Dad. I miss them."

"Me too," Tash said softly. Just thinking about her parents made her want to cry. But she was the older sister and couldn't cry in front of Zak. "Uncle Hoole's our family now."

Zak sulked. "Not really. He's—"

"Not even human," Tash finished.

"Yeah, and he's—"

"Only related to us because his brother married Aunt Beryl."

"Right," said Zak. "I don't even—"

"Know why he bothered to take us in?"

"Stop that!" Zak glared at his sister. She had an annoying habit of finishing other people's sentences.

"Sorry," his sister replied. She hadn't noticed she was doing it again. "But we've talked about Uncle Hoole before. He's not human—he's a Shi'ido. They believe all their relatives are part of their close family. So Hoole felt that he had to take us in when . . ." She could hardly say it. "When Mom and Dad died. We should be happy we get to live with someone who cares about us."

"He never shows it. He always looks like he's going to a funeral."

"You're just too hard on him." Tash argued harder than she believed. "He can be very friendly."

"Oh, yeah?" Zak huffed. "Then what's his first name?"

"Well, that's easy, his name is . . . I mean, I'm sure I've heard him . . . That is . . ." She stopped. Now that she thought about it, Uncle Hoole never had told them his first name. "Maybe he doesn't have a first name," she decided. "Maybe he's just Hoole."

"Maybe," Zak said with a sudden gleam in his eyes, "he just doesn't want us to know. Maybe it's something secret. Maybe there's a price on his head!"

"Zak Arranda, your imagination is galactic."

"Maybe he's part of the Rebellion and that's why he moves around so much."

11

Tash was growing impatient. "Bring it in for a landing, Zak. He's an anthropologist. He goes to different planets to study the species that live there."

"Sure, that's what he tells us. But if that's all there is, why does he keep his name a secret? I'm going to find out."

"How are you going to do that?"

"Easy. I'll check his cabin." Zak turned to go.

"You can't do that! It's rude. Besides, what if he finds you?"

"He won't find me," Zak said. "He's in the ship's library, doing research. He's *always* in the ship's library, doing research." Zak turned to go. "Want to help?"

"No," Tash said firmly. "It's not something a Jedi Knight would do."

"You're *not* a Jedi Knight."

"I'm still not going."

"Come on. It's not as though I'm going to dig through his personal files. I'm just going to glance at his desk to see if his name is on anything."

His sister shook her head. "I'm going back to the cockpit to practice my piloting."

"Suit yourself." Zak turned and hurried down the hall.

Tash frowned after him. At least she had gotten him to think about something besides their parents.

Now if someone could just do the same for her.

While Tash headed toward the cockpit, Zak crept toward the ship's living quarters. The last cabin belonged to Uncle Hoole. Zak pressed the caller.

No answer.

Zak pressed the opener and the door slid back with a soft *whoosh!*

And Zak found himself staring into the face of a fanged and drooling monster. Its bulk filled the doorway, and it was so close that Zak could smell its hot, stinking breath.

He cried out and stumbled backward, tripping over his own feet and falling to the ground. The creature lunged forward and bent over him. One clawed hand reached for his throat.

CHAPTER

The creature grabbed Zak's shirt and pulled him to his feet. "What are you doing here!" it demanded in a voice like sliding gravel.

"I—I . . . ," Zak stammered. He could feel the creature's putrid breath on his face.

The creature paused. It let go of Zak's shirt and took a step back. Then, before Zak's eyes, its flesh began to quiver and crawl. The monster's entire body squirmed and changed shape. After only a few seconds, it had transformed into something close to human. But its dark gray skin and extra-long fingers revealed it to be quite different.

"Uncle Hoole," Zak gasped. "It's you."

"You are in my cabin," Hoole said sternly. "Who else would you find here?"

Zak's knees were still shaking, but he felt relieved. He should have known this would happen eventually. Uncle Hoole was a Shi'ido. Although they looked mostly human, Shi'ido were aliens with a very nonhuman ability: They could change shape.

"Sorry," he said with one final shudder. "I just didn't . . . I mean, I've never seen you do that before. What *was* that thing you turned yourself into?"

Hoole turned his back on Zak and began to examine a small datapad. "A creature I observed in my travels. It keeps my shape-changing skills in practice," he replied.

"Practice for what?"

Hoole's gaze was like a blaster bolt. "For eating annoying small boys."

Tash believed it was her job as the older sister to make things easier for Zak, but she missed her parents terribly. She remembered the day she heard they were dead: She felt so lost and alone that she thought she'd go crazy.

The truth was, although she missed Alderaan, the only people she really missed were her parents. Tash had always had trouble making friends—other kids thought she was weird because she was always finishing their sentences or making predictions about what day a pop quiz was going to be held or getting strange feelings about things. Usually they were sad or frightening

15

things. Like the day her parents died. She knew it had happened even though she was light-years away. She felt like something was suddenly torn out of her. That had been the worst time, but not the first time.

When she had heard the news, Tash had wanted to lock herself in her room forever. But Zak wouldn't let her. He was just as sad and scared as she was, but he showed it in a different way. He stopped being afraid of anything. He became a daredevil, risking his neck on silly stunts like skimboarding, his current dangerous hobby. Tash knew he needed someone to watch over him. And she found to her surprise that she actually *liked* the little womp rat.

So instead of closing herself off from the galaxy, Tash had decided to face it with him.

And she had made a promise to herself that she would never lose anyone close to her ever again.

Tash entered the *Lightrunner*'s cockpit, with all its delicate instruments and gauges. The pilot and copilot's seats were empty, because the *Lightrunner* was operating on automatic.

Tash slid into the pilot's seat. She double-checked to make sure the navigational systems were securely locked on automatic, then grabbed the two levers that controlled the main thrusters.

In her mind she saw an image far sharper than any holographic projection. The Imperial battle station was surrounded by a gauntlet of TIE fighters, itching to test themselves against a young Jedi Knight.

Lost in her imagination, Tash was eager to meet their challenge.

Zak hadn't given up on Uncle Hoole. In fact, staring at Uncle Hoole's back while the anthropologist pored over his work, Zak became angry.

It wasn't fair. Hoole had volunteered to take them, but he refused to tell them anything about himself. He didn't even tell them where they were going. That bothered Zak, and he knew it bothered his sister, too. For the last six months, Hoole had dragged them all across the galaxy on his research, but he never explained what he was doing.

"Where are we headed?" Zak finally demanded.

Hoole looked up from his work. He scowled at Zak. "Are you still here? Oh, very well. The planet is called D'vouran. Does it mean anything to you?"

"No."

"Then go away."

"What are you going to do there?" Zak asked.

Hoole was exasperated. He handed Zak his computerized datapad. "Read this file. But *only* this file!"

The file Zak read told him the planet's story.

D'vouran was a typical life-bearing planet: tree-covered continents, salty blue oceans, and fresh, breathable air. According to rumor, it was the richest and most beautiful planet within a thousand light-years. It was inhabited by creatures who called themselves Enzeen. They were intelligent and very friendly. Considering the hundreds of magnificent unstudied planets in the galaxy, D'vouran didn't seem worth an anthropologist's time. Except for one thing.

No one had ever noticed it before.

D'vouran was less than a light-year from one of the galaxy's busiest space lanes, and yet it had never appeared on anyone's star charts. One day the planet wasn't there, and the next day it *was*.

"That's impossible, of course," Hoole said as Zak finished reading. "Planets do not just appear out of nowhere. It's a mistake in the star charts."

"Oh." Without thinking, Zak pressed Next on the datapad, and a new file popped onto the screen. He saw the words IMPERIAL ORDERS and PAYMENT RECEIVED just as Hoole·snatched the pad from his hand.

"I told you to read nothing else!"

"Sorry, I was just—"

"You were just snooping," Hoole interrupted. "Don't ever snoop in my cabin again." The Shi'ido turned back toward Zak, towering frighteningly over him. "If you do, you will be very, very sorry."

Hoole took another step forward and Zak gulped. Whatever Hoole planned to do next, he never got the chance. Both he and Zak were thrown to the floor by a sudden jolt. The *Lightrunner* shuddered and groaned as though some giant force had grabbed hold of it. Over the scream of the engines, Zak heard his uncle cry, "We're out of control!"

CHAPTER

Zak and Uncle Hoole rushed to the cockpit, stumbling every time the ship shuddered. When they reached the pilot's room, Tash was still sitting at the controls, her knuckles white with fear and her eyes wide.

"I didn't do anything!" she said in a panic. "I didn't touch anything!"

Through the viewport, they could see that the white blur of hyperspace was gone. They were in realspace, and the *Lightrunner* was plunging toward a blue-green planet.

Uncle Hoole's jaw tightened as he looked at Tash. "Move."

She scrambled out of the way as Hoole slipped into the pilot's chair and began to work the controls at a frantic pace. Deevee came up last, his gyros struggling to maintain their balance. The droid dropped into the copilot's chair and began to help his master.

"We're going to crash!" Zak shouted.

The planet surface was rushing up to meet them. Hoole's hands flew across the *Lightrunner*'s control panels. At first nothing changed—they continued to plummet as the planet grew larger and larger. But their uncle hit one last button and pulled back on the control stick, and the *Lightrunner* pulled out of its nosedive.

"I didn't touch anything I wasn't supposed to," Tash said in a small voice.

"What happened?" Zak asked.

Uncle Hoole pointed to an indicator light. "The ship has been dragged out of hyperspace."

Zak and Tash still had a lot to learn about astrophysics, but they understood the principles of space travel as well as they understood basic math. Starships used two different types of engines. Hyperdrives propelled vessels through an alternate dimension known as hyperspace, which allowed them to travel great distances in a short period. These powerful engines only worked in the absence of gravity. When on or near a planet, starships used their slower sublight engines.

Hoole continued, "I told the navicomputer to plot a course that would automatically take us out of hyperdrive just before we reached the planet D'vouran. But . . ."

"But what?" Zak asked.

Hoole double-checked his readouts. "We seemed to have arrived at our destination fifteen minutes ahead of schedule."

Zak said, "And D'vouran's gravity yanked the *Lightrunner* right out of hyperspace!"

Tash studied the innocent-looking blue-green planet. "You mean that planet tried to suck us in?"

Zak rolled his eyes. "Please, it's only gravity, Tash. Uncle Hoole, it's got to be a mistake in the navicomputer. Either that or the planet moved."

Hoole did not take his eyes off his instruments. "Planets do not change course. And there's nothing wrong with the navicomputer." He spared a brief, irritated glance at Tash. "Most likely the instruments were interfered with."

"I didn't touch anything I wasn't supposed to," Tash repeated.

But Hoole wasn't satisfied. "You were in here daydreaming again. This is a working starship, not a place for you to pretend you're a Jedi Knight."

Tash muttered, "Sorry," and looked down at her shoes.

Hoole ignored her apology. "Buckle yourselves in. The ride down will not be smooth."

That was an understatement. The sublight engines threatened to fail with every passing moment, and the ship's stabilizers had shorted. As they descended through D'vouran's gravity, every bolt in the *Lightrunner*'s frame shrieked at the strain. Through it all, Uncle Hoole remained cool and collected. Only the tightness in his jaw and his furrowed brow revealed his concern.

"Are we going to make it?" Zak asked as the *Lightrunner*'s engines sputtered.

Hoole didn't answer.

Through the observation port, Tash saw clouds roll back and, beneath them, a green forest laid out like a blanket. In the distance, a white spot appeared, growing steadily larger. The ship groaned as Hoole banked toward it.

"Is that a spaceport?" Zak said. "It looks more like a junk heap."

The *Lightrunner* did not fall apart. The engines kept them aloft as Hoole guided the ship onto the small launch deck. As the massive repulsors took over, lowering the cruiser clumsily to the tarmac, Hoole sighed with relief. But then the *Lightrunner* gave one final shudder and the engines died.

"That is not encouraging," Hoole said. "We should look at the engines."

"All right!" yelled Zak, a born tinkerer. "Let's go, Tash."

"Right behind you."

Tash was still sulking after the near accident. She was sure she hadn't damaged anything on the ship. She had

23

been daydreaming about the Jedi Knights, but she didn't deserve to be scolded for it.

Because she was still surly, she lagged behind her brother on his way to the exit. She would rather have a tooth pulled than look at a starship engine. By the time she had unbuckled her crash webbing, Zak and Uncle Hoole had lowered the ramp and were outside.

The moment Tash reached the door, a hole opened up in the pit of her stomach. She was overcome by a feeling of dread—as though some terrible evil was looming right before her eyes, staring at her, about to pounce on her. She had gotten such a feeling once before—on the day her parents died. She shivered.

But there was nothing there. She peeked out the hatch, but all she saw was the spaceport's landing pad and the blue sky above it. Still, the feeling lingered. Something was out there.

"Zak? Uncle Hoole?" she whispered. "Deevee?"

No answer.

Tash crept out of the *Lightrunner*'s door. The spaceport was very quiet. Most star ports were crowded with ships coming and going, workers unloading cargo, pilots hurrying to and from dozens of flight decks, and maintenance droids busily trying to repair the wear and tear of constant arrivals and departures. Not this place. D'vouran's spaceport looked deserted, and there were only a few ships on its flight deck. All of them looked like flying junk heaps—the thrown-together ships of poor travelers on the move.

The feeling of being watched was still there.

Tash took another step out. Where was her brother? "Zak?" she whispered . . .

. . . As something cold and slimy dropped around her neck.

CHAPTER

"Aaaagh!" she cried, pulling at the thing that grabbed her. It was soft and squishy, and when she yanked, it broke away. Tash saw that her hand was full of flowers.

"Nice going, Tash," Zak laughed, stepping around the side of the ship with Deevee beside him. He and Deevee both had necklaces of flowers around their necks. "I'm sure the Enzeen really appreciate you tearing their gifts apart."

Zak pointed at a person standing right beside Tash. She had been too nervous to see the man—well, not a man exactly. He was definitely humanlike, except that he had blue skin, and instead of hair, the top of his head was covered with short needlelike spines. He was plump, with chubby fingers and a round face covered mostly by a very friendly smile. He was holding a pile of flowered hoops. "Welcome to D'vouran. I am Chood, an Enzeen."

"N-Nice to meet you," Tash stammered. "Sorry about the, um . . ."

"Friendship necklace," Chood finished pleasantly. "That's quite all right. Have another." He hung another flower necklace around her neck.

"The Enzeen use these to welcome people to their planet," explained Deevee, coming up closer from around the side of the ship. "A nuisance, if you ask me."

"If you'd come out with us, you wouldn't have been so surprised," Zak added.

"Where were you?" Tash asked. "I called your name."

Zak pointed toward the tail end of the ship. "Sorry. Uncle Hoole had opened up the exterior panels to the lateral stabilizer, and I went with him to watch. I've never seen the inside of an ion thruster before."

"Thrilling," Deevee said, sounding as sarcastic as a droid could.

Uncle Hoole appeared, wiping oil from his hands and frowning even more than usual. "The damage is severe. Chood, is there anyone on D'vouran who can help us repair our ship?"

The Enzeen looked sympathetic. "I'm sorry. We Enzeen are not great travelers, and we don't know much about starships. In fact, we have very little use for any technology. However, there are several starpilots on the planet who may be able to help. Most of them spend time at the local cantina."

"Excellent," Hoole said. "Would you take us there?"

The Enzeen bowed low. "I would be honored to assist."

Chood led them down a flight of wide stairs and out of the spaceport. Just outside the exit stood a large sign in Basic, the common language most species in the galaxy used. It read: WELCOME TO D'VOURAN. OUR GOAL IS TO SERVE.

"Now that's a friendly sign," Zak said.

"I guess," Tash responded glumly.

Her brother leaned closer and whispered. "What's the matter with you? This Chood is doing his best to make us welcome here, and you look like someone's planning your funeral."

"I can't help it," she whispered back. "I just have a bad feeling about this place."

"You *always* have bad feelings," he muttered.

Chood led them through a little town next to the spaceport. It seemed primitive to Zak and Tash. They saw no vehicles, and most of the houses were small, one-story structures made of mud. They passed several people. Most of them were human, but there were some

28

aliens among them. Every now and then they would see another Enzeen, and Tash noticed that they all looked very much like Chood, with chubby blue bodies, spikes on their heads, and wide, friendly smiles. Each Enzeen they saw stopped to say hello and welcome them to D'vouran, as though they were old friends.

"Is this the whole town?" Zak snorted. "There's not even a good skimboard run!"

"This is it," Chood said. "There are a few homes closer to the forest, but most of the houses are here, in town. It's more like a village really."

Chood cheerfully explained the recent history of D'vouran. Ever since it was "discovered" by outsiders, the Enzeen had encouraged people to come to the planet. "There aren't many of us Enzeen," he explained. "And we don't like to travel. Inviting others to D'vouran is our way of learning about the galaxy."

"How was D'vouran discovered?" Zak asked.

"A cargo ship," Chood answered. "It wasn't expecting D'vouran to be here and was surprised by the planet's gravity. It crashed. When a rescue flight from offworld came to investigate, they discovered our planet, and our hospitality. The word spread from there."

Tash noticed that Uncle Hoole wasn't asking questions. So she decided to ask one of her own. "Were there any survivors of the original crash?"

29

Chood paused. "Only one. The rest died in the crash."

"Have many settlers come here since then?" Zak asked. "I mean, this place sounds pretty boring."

"Zak!" Tash scolded.

But Chood didn't seem offended. At least his smile never wavered. "There are a few hundred here. It's not a bad start for a planet that still hasn't been put on the official star maps. But there will be more. D'vouran has perfect weather and plenty of natural resources. We expect to have thousands before too long."

"Don't you worry about D'vouran becoming overcrowded?" Tash added.

"Oh, no," the Enzeen replied cheerily. "We enjoy it. We could never get our fill of visitors."

He led them down a short dead-end street. At the end of the street was a squat building with a wide-open door. Loud noise—music mixed with laughter and shouting—came from inside. A sign over the door revealed the cantina's name: THE DON'T GO INN. Tash and Zak both laughed when they saw the sign.

So far, Chood told them, most of the settlers who had come to D'vouran were explorers and treasure-seekers, hoping to strike it rich on an uncharted planet. "But," he added, "we are encouraging families like you to join our happy planet. D'vouran is paradise."

At that moment, someone came flying through the

Don't Go Inn's front door, landing face-first in the dusty street.

"Do you think *he* feels that way?" Zak joked.

"I'm afraid," Chood admitted, "we also have our share of ruffians."

"And there they are," Deevee noted.

A crowd of thugs poured out of the Don't Go Inn. They stood on the cantina's porch, jeering down at the man they had just thrown into the street.

"And stay outta here, Bebo!" one man called.

"Stop coming around here with your crazy stories!" another yelled. "We're tired of hearing about invisible monsters!"

"Yeah," snarled another, "we don't need you causin' us problems!" They hurled a few more insults and warnings at their victim before fading back into the shadows of the cantina.

Tash bent down next to the man, who had just crawled to his knees. "Are you all right?"

"They won't listen!" the man croaked. "They just won't listen."

His clothes were filthy rags. His hair was gray under a layer of dirt, and his beard was ragged and thin. He looked like a wild man who had just come out of the wilderness.

"I'll listen," Tash offered.

The man glanced at her suspiciously. He clutched his

31

worn shirt collar. "I won't have you mock me, too! I'm safe enough! I don't have to try to help them or anyone!"

Tash looked at Chood. "Do you know what he's talking about?"

"Pay him no attention," Chood said apologetically. "His name is Bebo. He is harmless, but not completely rational."

The wild man, Bebo, stared at Tash. "I should bring Lonni. They may believe her. Yes, that's it. But I don't think she'll come. She's too afraid. But I've got to try. Yes. That's what I'll do. Lonni."

The man got to his feet and walked off, still muttering to himself.

"I'd say he's a few starships short of a fleet," Zak said.

Chood pointed at the door. "This is the cantina I told you about," Chood explained. "I'm afraid the Don't Go Inn is not the nicest place on D'vouran, but you did want to find a starpilot who could help with your ship. Also, inside you will find all the free food you can eat. Compliments of the Enzeen."

Zak's eyes lit up. "Free food! I like this place already."

"It will do," Hoole said. "Thank you for your help."

"Please consider yourselves our honored guests on

D'vouran. If there is anything we can do, please let me know."

"There is one more thing," the Shi'ido replied. "I will be conducting some . . . business . . . starting tomorrow. Zak and Tash will need a place to stay, under the supervision of their caretaker, Deevee." Deevee stifled an electronic screech.

Chood held up one hand. "Please. Say no more. It would be an honor if they would stay with me. My house is not far from here."

"What!" Tash cried. "Uncle Hoole, you never said you were going to leave us!"

Hoole said calmly, "I have anthropological research to do, Tash. I will have no time to watch over you."

"But . . . but you're going to *leave* us!" she said.

"It won't take long," her uncle promised. "You can obviously rely on Chood, here, and you'll have Deevee. What could be the problem?"

Tash's mouth tightened into a thin straight line. How could she explain it? How could Hoole not understand? Her parents had left them in a stranger's care, and then they died. Now Hoole was doing the same thing. And that feeling of being watched still bothered Tash. But she knew she wouldn't be able to make Hoole understand, so instead she said nothing.

Hoole turned back to Chood. "Then it's settled. Again, I thank you."

Chood bowed. "Our goal is to serve." He told them where he lived, and turned away.

Tash and Zak had been in cantinas before, but never any place like this. Instead of a brightly lit room where people could see what they were eating and drinking, the Don't Go Inn was dark and smoky. Tash couldn't tell how many people were inside because everyone kept to the shadows. Half of them whispered to each other, while the other half shouted loudly around sabacc tables or at the bar.

Once their eyes adjusted to the gloom, Zak and Tash could make out some of the figures in the bar. Most of them were human, but there were a few other species mixed in. They recognized a horn-headed Devaronian, and a wolf-headed Shistavanen, and a gigantic Wookiee towering over a few humans in a corner. Hands, or tentacles, or flippers were wrapped around mugs filled with alien drinks. Every drinker had the hard look of someone who'd been in a lot of fights, and was looking for another one.

The newcomers were about to sit at a small table when a voice boomed, "Hoole!" At the same time, Tash felt a huge hand grab her by the shirt and slam her against a wall.

Someone was pointing a blaster right between her eyes.

CHAPTER

The hand and arm that held the blaster were almost as big as Tash, and the body they were attached to was even bigger. Looking up, Tash recognized the square, ugly face of a Gank.

A Gank *killer,* as they were usually called. She could see why. Its square yellow face was twisted into a permanent snarl, topped by cruel beady eyes. Its massive shoulders looked like small hills, and its arms were as thick as tree trunks. Ganks usually worked as hired guns and bodyguards for rich crime lords. Why had this one decided to pick on her?

Tash got her answer in the next moment. The cantina had fallen silent and still as everyone watched and waited to see what was going to happen next. Out of the corner of her eye, Tash saw that Zak, too, had been grabbed, and there was a blaster pointed at his head as well. Someone was even pointing a blaster at Deevee. Only Uncle Hoole had not been touched. He stood face-to-face with the most disgusting creature Tash had ever seen. It was a giant slug, with two pudgy arms sticking out of its fat, fleshy body. Slobber trickled from the edges of its wide mouth when it talked. It was this creature that had yelled Hoole's name. A moment later, Tash learned who the creature was.

Smada the Hutt.

"Hoole!" Smada the Hutt bellowed again. "What a pleasant surprise this is."

"Tell your thugs to let my niece and nephew go, Smada," Hoole said in a low voice.

"No," the slimy Hutt replied. "Not until we've had a chance to talk. And by the way, the minute you use any of your shape-changing powers, my bodyguards will blast your small friends to bantha fodder."

"Leave us alone!" Zak demanded.

"What do you want?" Tash called out.

Smada the Hutt's flesh jiggled as he chuckled and looked at Tash. "Simple. I want your uncle to work for me. I have need of an assassin to eliminate some of my enemies, and Hoole's shape-changing powers will make him the perfect weapon."

36

"You're crazy!" Tash replied. "Uncle Hoole's a scientist, not a killer!"

Smada the Hutt laughed. "Ho, ho! Is that so? Well, I'd say there's a lot about your uncle that you don't know."

Tash was taken aback. What did he mean by that?

"You are wasting your time, Smada," Hoole said. "What are you doing on this backwater planet anyway?"

Smada wiped a line of drool from his fat face. "Gang wars on my home planet have made it necessary for me to take a short vacation."

"You mean *hide,* I'll bet," Zak interrupted.

Smada continued. "In fact, those gang wars are the reason I need a new assassin. Until I found one, this new planet seemed like the perfect place to lie low for a while." Smada leaned forward until his putrid face was only a few inches from Hoole's. "And I was right. Because a stroke of luck brought you here, too. And now you will work for me."

Hoole shook his head. "I told you no the last time we met, Smada."

The Hutt growled. "And I told you that no one defies Smada the Hutt. I also told you that if we ever met again, I wouldn't ask so nicely. So if you don't agree to work for me right now, I'll have your little brats vaporized."

37

Suddenly a tall man stepped out of the shadows, pointing a well-worn blaster at Smada. "I don't think so," he said.

"This is none of your concern, stranger," Smada growled.

The tall man answered with a cocky grin. "I'm making it my business."

"And mine," said a young woman, who appeared beside the man.

"And mine," said another man with blond hair. He ignited a strange, glowing weapon that looked like a sword made of pure energy. Tash gasped. A Jedi *lightsaber*!

"And his," said the tall man, pointing to the huge Wookiee Tash had seen before. The furry Wookiee let out a threatening roar.

If looks had been lasers, Smada would have incinerated them all. But he obviously didn't want to fight. "D'vouran is a small planet, Hoole. We'll meet again."

Smada signaled to his thugs, who freed Zak and Tash. Tash saw that Smada had been sitting on a hoversled, a long platform that floated in the air. With his bodyguards around him, Smada the Hutt floated out of the cantina. Since there was nothing left to watch, the rest of the cantina patrons went back to their business, and the noise resumed.

The tall man and the woman holstered their blasters,

while the blond man deactivated his lightsaber. Behind them hovered two droids, a stocky R2 unit and a golden protocol droid.

"Oh, what a relief! I was about to short circuit!" the droid said. "Shouldn't we notify the authorities?"

"Pipe down, Threepio," the tall man said. "There aren't any authorities on D'vouran. Just the Enzeen, and they're too friendly to do much about Smada." He looked at Hoole. "Everyone okay?"

"Yes," Hoole said. "Luckily Smada was more interested in making threats than hurting anyone. Thank you for your help."

"What was that all about?" Tash asked her uncle.

"He seemed to know you," the young man with the lightsaber observed.

Hoole hesitated. Finally he said cautiously, "Yes. He . . . offered me a job several years ago. When I refused to accept, he swore that he would have his revenge. It was a coincidence that brought us together on this planet."

"An unhappy one, I'd say," the woman added. "That Smada's pretty foul-tempered, even for a Hutt."

"I've known worse," the tall man said.

The Shi'ido introduced himself. "My name is Hoole."

"I'm Han Solo. Call me Han," said the tall man. He had the casual confidence of a starpilot. "This is my partner, Chewbacca," he added, indicating the Wookiee. Then he pointed at the woman. "And this is—"

"Princess Leia," Tash finished.

The woman blinked. All the newcomers looked around to make sure no one had overheard. Han Solo's hand crept toward the blaster slung low on his hip.

The young man with the lightsaber saw the movement and said, "It's all right, Han."

But Han growled, "I'm not taking any chances."

The woman, Leia, gently put her hand over Han's. "Let me handle this." To Tash, she said, "What makes you think that's my name?"

Zak shook his head. "It's gotta be. Tash is always right about stuff like that. It's weird."

Tash said, "It's not so weird! Zak and I live on Alderaan, where you're from. I mean, we did . . . before it . . . well, you know."

She could see from the woman's face that Leia knew very well what had happened to Alderaan.

Beside her, Zak almost shouted, "Hey, are you guys *Rebels?*"

"Zak!" Tash hissed.

Han's face turned to a scowl. "We're minding our own business, kid, which is what you should be doing."

"We're . . . researchers," Leia interrupted gently. "We're looking this planet over for some friends of ours. We were just about to leave, but we couldn't sit back and let that Hutt threaten you."

Tash heard Uncle Hoole reply, "I am a researcher, too." But she remembered the Hutt's words: *There's a lot about your uncle that you don't know.*

There's a lot about everyone *I don't know,* Tash thought. Leia had been a princess on Alderaan. Whatever she was doing with these people was a lot more important than "research."

"Maybe," Tash said hesitantly, "we could sit down for a while. You could tell us about your *research—*"

"Of course we will," Leia interrupted with a quick glance at Han. "We'll stay at least until we're sure that Hutt doesn't come back around."

The two parties sat down together. Han Solo propped his feet up on an empty chair. "Order anything you want. The food's free you know. These Enzeen will feed you till you're ready to burst."

Uncle Hoole nodded. "We've only met one, but he seems extremely friendly."

To Zak's delight, they did order food from a passing waiter. Moments later the Enzeen reappeared with plates piled high with all sorts of exotic meats, pastries, and fruits. Zak wrinkled his nose at a dish full of eight-legged insects covered in a pink sauce. But when he dipped a finger into the sauce and tasted it, his eyes lit up and he began shoveling it in. The only one at the table who kept up with him was the Wookiee.

Tash had no appetite. Her stomach was in a knot—the feeling of fear had not gone away. She was trying to ignore it. It was probably just her imagination anyway, and she refused to make a fool of herself the way she'd done when the Enzeen put the flowers around her neck.

As they began to eat, everyone relaxed. Even Han Solo seemed to be interested as Uncle Hoole and Zak described their journey. But Tash drifted from one conversation to another, unable to concentrate. Deevee had been cornered by C-3PO and his companion, R2-D2.

". . . and then I found myself alone on the planet Tatooine, wandering through that terrible desert!" Threepio was saying. "It was perfectly dreadful."

"Fascinating, I'm sure," Deevee replied. He looked as bored as a droid could look.

"Wait until you hear what happened next!" Threepio trilled.

"I don't suppose you were deactivated or anything convenient like that?" Deevee asked.

"Well, no."

"Too bad," the unhappy droid muttered. "Well, you might as well go on, then, . . ."

Tash could barely pay attention. Maybe it was the exotic food, or maybe the feeling of being watched was growing stronger, but she thought she might be sick. The sensation was so strong that she had actually forgotten about the blond man with the Jedi lightsaber, until he leaned across the table to speak to her.

"Is everything all right?" he asked.

"Um, yeah. Fine," she said.

The young man smiled. "Your name's Tash, right? I'm Luke. Luke Skywalker."

Something about him made her feel strange. Not "strange" like the crushes she'd had on boys back on Alderaan—she had outgrown crushes anyway. This was a sense of . . . relief. Tash felt as if she'd been waiting to meet someone like Luke Skywalker all her life.

His blue eyes stared at her like a scanner reaching into her deepest thoughts. "Something's troubling you."

"I guess," Tash began. She never liked telling people about the feelings she sometimes got. But she found herself confiding in him easily. "I guess I feel a little uneasy here. I don't know what exactly, but something's bothering me. It's probably just my imagination." She didn't expect him to understand, since no one ever understood.

To her surprise, Luke said, "Not too long ago, a good friend taught me a very important lesson: trust your feelings."

From the next chair, Chewbacca barked a question at Hoole, and Han translated. "So you say you dropped out of hyperspace fifteen minutes too early?"

43

"Uncle Hoole nodded. "It caused a great deal of damage to our ship."

"The same thing happened to us. My ship, the *Millennium Falcon,* got shaken up pretty good." The starpilot shook his head. "I don't know, maybe it's just an error in the star charts."

"Perhaps," Uncle Hoole agreed. "But in our case, I think it was some problems we had on board." He glared at Tash.

Zak laughed. "He means Tash. She was playing Jedi Knight in the cockpit."

Tash felt her face grow red. Luke Skywalker raised an eyebrow and gave her a knowing smile. "So you want to be a Jedi, do you?"

"I've read about them," she confessed. "My parents were on Alderaan when it . . . you know. I always thought that if there were more Jedi, they wouldn't have let it happen."

"They do their best, Tash," Luke said. "That's all any of us can do."

"Are—are you a Jedi?" she asked almost in a whisper, pointing at his lightsaber.

Luke shook his head. "I wish I could say yes. But no, I'm not. This lightsaber belonged to my father."

Tash nodded sadly. "They say all the Jedi are gone now. So I don't know how I'd ever find one to teach me."

Luke put his hand on her shoulder. He whispered,

"Don't give up hope yet. You might be surprised. A Jedi might come looking for you someday."

Tash wanted to know what he meant by that. But she didn't get a chance to ask. Because at that moment, someone screamed.

CHAPTER

The scream came from outside, somewhere near the cantina. Most of the patrons looked up just long enough to make sure they were in no danger, then ignored the cries. They had come to this new planet to escape trouble, not to find it.

But everyone at Tash's table jumped up and ran toward the door. The cries were coming from behind the cantina. Their new friends—Tash was now sure they were Rebels, because they acted with so much courage—drew their weapons.

But the street was deserted except for the wild man, Bebo. He was on his knees, scratching at the dirt and shouting. "No! No! No!"

Tash was not afraid of Bebo. "What's wrong?" she asked him.

"She's gone! She's gone!" The madman croaked. "My friend Lonni was standing here a minute ago, and she just vanished!"

"What do you mean 'vanished'?" Hoole asked.

Bebo stood up. The light in his eyes had become fierce. "I mean vanished! Gone! Disappeared! And it's all my fault! I convinced her to come out of hiding. To warn everyone! They didn't believe me, but they might believe her. She came because I told her she'd be safe! But she's gone. She was standing here, and then she wasn't!"

Although no one from the cantina had come out, a few settlers had come to investigate the shouting. These people were a more wholesome-looking crowd, Tash noted. Probably the families and pioneers Chood had mentioned. But they seemed as uninterested in Bebo's ravings as the cantina patrons. In fact, most of them were laughing.

Someone called out, "Go ahead, Bebo! Tell us another!"

"Yeah," someone added, "Tell us about vanishing people!"

"And invisible monsters!"

"Or was it invisible people and vanishing monsters?"

47

The crowd laughed at the joke. Chood appeared, and for a split second, Tash thought she saw the smile leave his face at the sight of Bebo. But it reappeared again, as bright as ever. "May I be of service?"

Tash pointed to Bebo. "He needs help. A friend of his disappeared."

Chood sighed. "I'm sorry if this has troubled anyone. Unfortunately Bebo has done this many times before. I assure you that no one has disappeared."

"Lonni disappeared!" Bebo's voice dropped into a whisper. "She was my only friend."

Tash felt something tug at her heart. She knew what it was like to lose someone.

One of the settlers called out, "You're crazy, Bebo!"

Chood nodded. "Sadly, it's true. Ever since he came here, poor Bebo has been ranting and raving about disappearances."

"It's true!" Bebo responded. "They died. The entire crew of the *Misanthrope*! They disappeared!"

Chood gazed sympathetically at Bebo, then turned to Hoole and the others and said softly, "This is a sad tale. The *Misanthrope* was the cargo ship that first crashed here. Bebo, here, was the captain and the only survivor. I'm afraid the guilt was too much for his mind. It snapped."

"No, no, no!" Bebo argued. "They disappeared. All of them!"

"He should be treated at a mental facility," observed Deevee.

"It's not that simple," Chood replied. "The official report said that he was responsible for the crash. If he leaves the planet, he'll be thrown into prison. But we Enzeen are a little more sympathetic, so we let him live here, despite the fact that he continually disrupts the environment we try to create for our settlers."

"Have you followed up on his claims that there were other survivors?" Hoole asked. "Who is this Lonni person he talks of?"

"There was a full investigation of the crash," the Enzeen replied. "And the Imperial officials declared no survivors. This person Bebo is raving about could not have lived."

"That's a lie!" Bebo snapped. "She was here!"

"Oh, really?" Chood said. His voice was still very calm and pleasant. "Then, please tell me, Bebo, where was your friend when she disappeared?"

Bebo pointed at the ground. "Right there! Right there! We were walking along, and *poof!* she was gone!"

"Walking along, you say? Are those your footprints, then?" Chood pointed at a line of footprints in the dirt road.

"Yes! That's where I was."

"Then where are your friend's footprints?" the Enzeen asked.

"Why they're right . . ." For the first time, Bebo stopped muttering to himself. There were no other footprints on the ground. There was no sign that anyone but Bebo had been standing there. "But she was right there! Right there!"

Chood shrugged. "You see. He is quite mad. It is most regrettable."

"Can't you help him? At least search the village?" Tash asked.

"We can, but we won't find anything," Chood says. "People who wish to be found on D'vouran are easy to find. Those who wish to hide, well, it's a large planet."

By this time, most of the settlers had lost interest and gone about their business. Uncle Hoole, too, wanted to move on. "Let's go, Tash," he said. "These people have offered to help us fix the *Lightrunner*, and we can't keep them waiting."

As the others turned away, Tash said softly to Bebo, "I'm sorry I can't help you. I wish there was something I could do for you."

Bebo gave her a cold, hard look. "It doesn't matter. Before long you'll be dead. You're all going to die."

CHAPTER

The look on Bebo's face still haunted Tash as she followed her brother and the others back to the spaceport. Han and Chewbacca examined the *Lightrunner*'s engines, and Han nodded confidently. "Don't worry. We'll have her asteroid-hopping in no time."

"He means it," Leia said. "If he can keep his own scrap pile in the air, he can sure handle your ship."

Han looked hurt. "The *Falcon* is the best ship in the galaxy." He pointed his finger at a saucer-shaped freighter across the landing bay.

"That's your ship?" Zak asked. "I thought it was a garbage scow."

"Zak!" Tash chided.

But Han had obviously met with this reaction before. "Tell you what, kid. You keep quiet for about half an hour while I work, and I'll show you some things about the *Falcon* that the Imperial engineers would love to get their hands on."

As they went to work, Tash paced about anxiously. She couldn't get Bebo's hurt, angry look out of her mind, and his voice whispered in her ear: *You're all going to die!*

Luke Skywalker appeared beside her. "Still have that feeling?"

"Yeah," she replied, once again surprised at his perceptiveness. "I couldn't help feeling sorry for Bebo. I don't know why, but I felt like he was telling the truth. I feel like I should check out his story."

Luke said seriously, "I meant what I said. You should trust your feelings."

She thought for a moment. "For what I want to do, I need to get on the HoloNet, and I can't do that until the *Lightrunner* is up and running again."

"Why not use the computer aboard the *Millennium Falcon*?" Luke offered.

A few minutes later, Tash was sitting at a cluttered computer station inside the battered freighter. She studied the computer setup. Han Solo wasn't kidding about modifications. Even the computer looked rigged.

"What's that?" she asked, pointing at a small black box attached to the computer terminal.

"I'm not sure," Luke said. "But I think it's a trace

detector. It signals you whenever someone is locking on to your computer signal."

"Why would you need that?" Tash asked.

Luke grinned. "Let's just say Han doesn't always work with the most trustworthy people."

Tash left it at that. Powering up the computer, she entered a few quick commands and logged onto the HoloNet News Service. Then she typed:

SEARCH REQUEST: MISANTHROPE.

The computer responded quickly.

SEARCH WORD MISANTHROPE RETURNED SIX HUNDRED ITEMS. DISPLAY ALL?

Tash groaned. That was far too many. She had to narrow down her search. She typed again.

SEARCH REQUEST: MISANTHROPE AND D'VOURAN.

The computer responded: TWO ITEMS FOUND. DISPLAY?

The first item looked like an official Imperial report. Tash displayed it. The report described the loss of the cargo ship and the subsequent search. She was hoping to find something in the report that might prove Bebo's story—that there had been survivors. But she lost hope as she read the report.

THE MISANTHROPE WENT DOWN WITH ALL HANDS ABOARD. ONLY THE PILOT, CAPTAIN KEVREB BEBO, SURVIVED. BEBO IS CURRENTLY WANTED FOR QUESTIONING, BUT IS AT LARGE.

She sighed. "Oh, well, I guess that's it, then. He really is mad from guilt."

The second file, oddly enough, was in code. "That's strange. Why would a news-service report be in code?"

"That's an Imperial code," Luke noted. "You'd better not mess with it."

Tash smirked. She started to enter signals, trying to break through the security system that kept her from reading the Imperial messages. But she had only entered a few commands when the little black box screeched an alarm.

"What's that?" she cried, almost jumping out of her seat.

Luke replied, "The trace detector! Someone's trying to track you down."

"What do I do?" she asked in a panic. The alarm grew louder.

"Shut it down!"

She slapped the Off key. The computer screen faded to black, and the alarm cut off. Tash felt her heart flutter. "What was that all about?"

"I don't know," Luke said. "But obviously the Empire wants to know about anyone asking questions about D'vouran."

Tash and Luke returned to the *Lightrunner* to find Chewbacca sitting with Zak, who was tinkering with a flat board. It was a little over one meter long and a half meter wide, and filled with intricate circuitry.

"Hey, Tash!" Zak said happily. "Chewbacca here is

helping me rewire my skimboard! It's going to be souped up fast enough to race a speeder bike!''

Nearby, Deevee said dryly, ''And I hope the Wookiee is prepared to pay your medical bills when you break your neck.''

Han wiped maintenance oil from his hands as he said to Hoole, ''That should do you for the short run. Your lateral stabilizer's damaged, and you'll need an overhaul, but the ship'll get you off planet.''

Hoole said his thanks as Han and his friends prepared to leave.

Tash said very shyly to Luke Skywalker, ''I didn't realize you were going so soon. I wanted to ask you about . . . about your lightsaber. And,'' her voice dropped to an embarrassed whisper. ''about the Force.''

He smiled warmly. ''I'm not sure how much I could tell you, Tash. But we may meet again some day and you and I can have a talk then.''

An electric tingle rose up Tash's hand as Luke shook it. The tingle lasted long after the *Millennium Falcon* had blasted into the sky.

It was growing dark by the time they left the spaceport for a second time. Following the directions they had been given, Uncle Hoole led them to Chood's house. The Enzeen lived in the forest, not far from the settlement.

Chood welcomed them warmly to his home. It was a

modest house, with three or four rooms connected by a long hallway. Although it was well built, Tash was surprised to find that, like the streets outside, the floor was uncovered, leaving only bare dirt.

"We have our traditions," Chood said when she noticed. "We like to keep in touch with the planet that is our home."

Chood certainly did love D'vouran. For an hour, Hoole, Tash, and Zak listened as he told them about the planet, singing the praises of its landscapes, its resources, its potential.

"He sounds," Zak whispered to Tash, "like a used landspeeder salesman."

Toward the end of the conversation, Tash found herself yawning. It had been a long, strange day—from their near crash to the incident in the cantina to meeting Luke Skywalker. She was tired. Beside her, Zak was nodding off.

Hoole noticed. "I think it is time for Zak and Tash to sleep. And time for me to be on my way."

"Where are you going?" Tash asked. She was so sleepy that she'd forgotten Hoole's usual secrecy about his work.

He reminded her instantly. "That is my affair. I will be back before morning. Excuse me."

Without another word, Hoole left.

"Don't Shi'ido ever sleep?" Zak yawned. "He's always running off somewhere."

"It's not because he's a Shi'ido," Tash replied. "It's just that he's Uncle Hoole, and there's more to him than meets the eye." *And,* she added to herself, *I'm going to find out what it is.*

Tash and Zak shared a large room where two small but comfortable sleeping mats lay on the floor. Once they were alone, Tash turned to her brother.

"I can't shake this feeling, Zak. Whatever I do, I feel like someone's watching me." She told him about the coded Imperial file about D'vouran, and the trace alert. "Suppose the Imperials know something about this planet that we don't?"

Zak had been nearly asleep. "Tash, I'm as mad at the Empire as you are. But what could they know about this planet that would be so bad? Don't you think you're taking this Jedi thing a little too far? It's like your looking for something to be wrong. This place is great!"

"You think having blasters pointed at you is great?"

"Yeah," he replied sleepily.

That's because you don't know any better, she wanted to say. But didn't. "I wish I had your confidence," she said instead.

"Just ease up on your thrusters and relax," he yawned. "Now excuse me. I wanna go skimboarding tomorrow, and I need my sleep."

Tash stayed awake longer. But finally she, too, fell asleep.

———

A sound woke her in the middle of the night. At first she thought it was Zak snoring, but her brother was sleeping quietly across the room. She could just make out the rise and fall of his chest as he breathed softly.

She listened carefully.

Slurp-slurp.

She listened more closely.

Slurp-slurp.

"Zak?" she whispered. "Do you hear that?"

No answer. Her brother was sound asleep.

Tash lay in bed, wondering what to do. The sound started, stopped, and started again several times. What could it be?

Finally she couldn't stand it anymore. Tash got up and crept to the door to their room. The sound was coming from inside the house.

Stealthily she opened the door and tiptoed into the hallway.

Slurp-slurp. Slurp-slurp.

The common room. That's where the sound came from. Tash crept forward, pressing flat against the wall. Her pulse raced, but something pushed her forward. Not curiosity, exactly. More like a terrible feeling that *not* knowing what it was would be more awful than finding out. Her heart pounded so loudly she was sure someone could hear it.

Slurp—

The sound stopped. She heard something shuffle

through the darkness of the common room. Tash gathered herself, then carefully peeked around the corner.

The room was empty.

"May I help you?"

Tash choked on the scream that tried to burst from her throat.

Chood was standing behind her. Even in the darkness, she could tell that he was still smiling.

"Um . . . I thought I heard something," she whispered.

"Stray animals, no doubt," the Enzeen explained. "We are near the edge of the forest here. I'm sure it was nothing. But would you like me to check?"

She paused. Was it her imagination, or was Chood staring at her in the darkness? In the shadows his smile looked more like an evil grin. "Don't trouble yourself," she replied.

"It's no trouble. I was going out anyway."

Tash couldn't help but ask, "This late?"

She thought she saw Chood's grin widen.

"I'm afraid so. An errand that will not wait."

"Okay. Well . . . thanks."

Chood bowed. "Our goal is to serve. Good night."

"Good night," she answered as she stumbled past him and headed back down the hall. She felt his eyes linger on her back. Then she heard a door close as he left the house.

"Relax," she told herself. "You'd probably stare at

someone, too, if you found them roaming around your house in the middle of the night.'' Wild animals. Well, it seemed as good an explanation as any.

You and your feelings *are getting out of hand, Tash Arranda,* she thought. *Maybe Zak's right. Maybe you are looking for problems. If you're not careful, you'll end up as crazy as Bebo.*

By the time she reached the door to the guest room, Tash had resolved not to jump to conclusions. Maybe Zak was right. She was too obsessed with the Force. Tash pushed the bedroom door open.

Someone was leaning over Zak's bed.

CHAPTER

A hand closed over Tash's mouth, stifling her shout.

So she bit the hand.

"Arrggh!" someone howled in pain, dropping Tash. The cry woke her brother, who sat bolt upright in bed. "Wh-what's going on?"

"Zak, look out!" Tash yelled. The shadowy figure was reaching down for him. Still half-asleep, Zak launched himself out of bed like an uncoiled spring, right past the shadowy figure.

"Run!" Tash yelled.

Even in the gloom, Tash recognized the two huge, square-shaped intruders: Ganks. The one she had bitten was still nursing his wounded hand. For good measure she stomped on his foot, then jumped through the door-way, with Zak close behind her.

"Help! Help!" she called. But there was no one to hear her. Uncle Hoole had gone to perform his mysterious work. Chood had gone on his errand. They were alone in the house.

"We've got to get out of here!" she told Zak, who was just barely awake. He followed her as she threw open the front door and ran outside.

The night air of D'vouran woke Zak up quickly. "What's back there?" he huffed as he ran to catch up with his sister.

"Smada! His thugs!" was all she could get out between gasps as she ran toward the center of town.

That was all Zak needed to know. His legs churned as he caught up to his sister. He didn't bother to look back.

Tash did, but she knew what she would see. The two Ganks were after them. For big, heavy brutes they ran quickly. Although Zak and Tash had already reached the main street of the small village, the two Ganks were gaining on them.

"Help! Help!" she shouted. But it was late at night, and the streets were deserted. A few lights went on in some of the houses, but Tash was afraid to stop. She could hear the heavy footsteps of the Ganks closing in.

She tried to lose them by veering sharply to the right, down a side street. Zak followed her.

Right to a dead end.

The Don't Go Inn loomed up before them. No time

to look back now. Without missing a beat, Tash raced up to the door and slapped the Open button.

It was locked.

"Open up!" she yelled, pounding on the door.

"Open up! Help!" Zak added.

Behind them, Tash heard two sudden howls. It sent shivers down her spine. The Ganks must be furious! They would tear her apart once they caught up. The cries were cut off sharply, but Tash was pounding the door so hard that she didn't notice.

"Open up! Please!" she begged. She expected any moment to feel the Gank's heavy hand on her throat, or feel the bite of a blaster bolt in her back. "Help!"

Finally the door flew open. A few startled settlers stumbled out, bleary-eyed and in bedclothes. "What's going on here?" one of them demanded.

"They're after us! Help!" Tash pleaded.

"Who's after you?" the settlers demanded.

"Them!" Tash said, pointing back down the street. But no one was there.

CHAPTER

Zak and Tash sat in the common room of Chood's home, where they had been sitting for almost an hour. It was still late at night, and Zak was nodding off in his seat. Even Tash yawned—the adrenaline that had pumped through her was long gone.

Hoole had returned—*from where?* Tash wondered—to find the village in an uproar. The whole town had been awakened by Tash and Zak's cries, only to find the story they heard as believable as one of Bebo's delusions.

Uncle Hoole had just finished apologizing to most of the settlers in the village, and to all of the Enzeen. Finally he sat down in front of Zak and Tash. His Shi'ido face was wrinkled into a tired frown.

"You two have managed to make us the most unpopular people in the village."

Tash, of course, had told him her story. There were Ganks. They had been chased. She had run up to the Don't Go Inn and pounded on the door. The next thing she knew, the Ganks had vanished.

"There were no Ganks," Hoole said. "You were having a dream."

"They were there!" Tash insisted. "They must have stopped chasing us when we yelled."

Hoole shook his head. "I checked. There weren't even any footprints. It was a dead-end street. Where would they have gone?"

"I don't know!"

"Tash." Hoole studied her closely. "The settlers at the Don't Go Inn said they saw only you and Zak screaming as though the entire planet was coming apart. No one else saw these Ganks."

"Zak did, didn't you, Zak?" She looked to her brother for support.

"Um . . . yeah. I guess."

"You guess?" Uncle Hoole interrogated.

Zak looked down. He wanted to help his sister, but . . . "Well, I was kind of asleep. I heard Tash yell 'Run!' so I ran. I mean, I think I saw something. I saw shadows. It was dark. I was sleeping. But there was probably something there."

Hoole shook his head. "Probably? Zak, look at it this way. Let's say Tash's story is the hyperdrive engine on a starship. And let's say what you saw is the motivator circuit. Now, if the engine is good, you connect the circuit and go to lightspeed. But if it's bad, the minute you plug in your circuit, the whole ship explodes. So you have to be sure." Hoole asked again. "Now, are you going to plug into that circuit?"

Zak hesitated, but only because he felt guilty. He struggled for something to say. "I'm sorry, Tash. I just . . . I was too sleepy. I didn't actually *see* anything."

"Zak!" Tash was almost in tears.

"Please don't cry, Tash," Hoole said. "No one is blaming you for anything. You just had a nightmare."

"It was real. I bit his nasty Gank finger!"

"You *dreamed* that you bit someone. It seemed so real that it made you walk—or rather, run—in your sleep. These things happen."

"No," she insisted stubbornly. "I was awake. I saw them. Why don't we find that Hutt and make him admit that he sent his thugs after us! Then ask him where they are now. He'll tell you they disappeared."

Hoole considered the option seriously. "That would be difficult. Smada has a small fortress just inside the forest. If we went there, I suspect we would not come out again. And I doubt Smada would confess to kidnapping just because we asked him."

Hoole sighed. "Actually, I blame myself. I know

how hard things must be for you since . . . the tragedy. I thought this interest in the Jedi would take your mind off your sadness. But now your imagination is running wild with this Jedi obsession. It's got to stop. First you upset the *Lightrunner*'s navicomputer. Then Chood tells me you were wandering around in the middle of the night, and now these dreams.'' The Shi'ido put one hand on Tash's shoulder. The gesture was clumsy, but she knew he meant well. ''Tash, you just have to understand that not everything in the galaxy is a great mystery. Some things are just what they appear to be. You don't need to wonder about the Force every time the wind blows. Do you understand?''

Tash looked up at the ceiling, then down at the dirt floor. Did she understand? She wasn't sure. Life was so confusing! Should she trust her feelings, or her common sense? Her feelings told her that she was in danger, that everyone was in danger. But her common sense told her that there was nothing out there to be afraid of, except a madman's stories and her own imagination. Besides Smada the Hutt, D'vouran appeared to be a peaceful planet.

Maybe she *was* looking too hard for mysteries in everything. Ever since her parents had died, she had felt angry. She didn't know who she was angry at, but she knew the feeling was real. Maybe this feeling of dread was just an excuse to be angry at *something*.

Her uncle waited for her to speak. Finally she said,

"All right, Uncle Hoole. You may be right. Maybe no one did disappear. But you'd better promise me one thing. You and Zak better not vanish."

Hoole almost cracked a smile. "I promise."

The sun rose early the next morning, and Zak Arranda rose with it. He couldn't sleep. Across the bedroom, Tash had finally crashed. After Hoole had talked with them, they'd gone back to bed. Even Hoole had gone to bed then, sleeping on a small cot in Chood's living room. But in their room, Zak had heard his sister lie awake, tossing and turning.

Zak wondered if he'd done the right thing. Had he told the truth or not? He just wasn't sure. And if there's one thing Zak hated, it was doubt. That's why he liked engines, circuits, and physics. When you were building an engine or charting a hyperspace course, you were either right or wrong. There weren't any gray areas. It didn't matter what you were *feeling*. You just double-checked your math and had your answer. If you were wrong, you tried again.

All this talk of shadows, sleep, and dreams made him nervous. He needed to do something. He wasn't like Tash, who could sit and think about a problem forever until she came up with an answer. Zak did his best thinking when he was on the move.

That's why he left Chood's house early the next

morning and went out onto the deserted streets of the village, carrying his skimboard.

The morning air was warm, fresh, and scented by the forest that surrounded the town. Zak understood why people had accepted the Enzeen's invitation to settle on D'vouran. It was beautiful.

Zak slid his skimboard out of its carrying case. Before starting the board's microengines, Zak put on his crash helmet, elbow pads, and knee pads. After all, as he had told Deevee a dozen times, he was a daredevil, but he wasn't stupid. Once he was padded up, Zak checked the stick-strips on the top of the board to make sure they were sticky enough to keep him in place.

The skimboard had many high-tech devices, but the most important were the lines of goo called stick-strips. Skimboard riders on Zak's home planet of Alderaan had been nicknamed slashers because of the stunts they pulled by "slashing" through the air, turning flips, and especially going vertical. That meant using the board's built-in anticollision system to fly toward a wall at top speed and then bank straight up. The slasher would be held in place only by the stick-strips that kept his feet connected to the board. Most slashers could get a two- or three-meter vertical ride before gravity caught up and pulled the board into its upright position. The all-time record for a vertical ride was five meters.

Zak planned to break it.

He laid the board on the ground and stepped onto it. The foot controls were near the back. Zak bent his knees for balance, then with a practiced swipe of his toe, he activated the repulsor lift.

His stomach dropped as the board sprang high into the air. Zak almost lost his balance, and the board wobbled beneath him, but he quickly righted himself.

Chewbacca's rewiring had worked well. Maybe *too* well. The skimboard was designed to hover an arm's length above the ground. Zak had wanted it to go a little higher, but now he found himself floating higher than even a Wookiee could reach. A fall from that height was not going to be fun. But Zak had no intention of letting that stop him. He had a vertical ride record to break.

Propelling himself forward, Zak skimmed through the air until he reached the Don't Go Inn. It was two stories tall. Even with the extra altitude of Zak's skimboard, the roof was at least six meters above his head. With a good run to gather speed, Zak and his souped-up board should be able to bank up the wall and get over the top with momentum to spare.

Tapping the accelerator, Zak leaned into a turn and skimmed away from the hotel, then whipped around and hovered. He had a twenty-meter runway straight to the white siding of the hotel. That should do it.

Taking a deep breath, he tapped the accelerator into full. The hot-wired skimboard rapidly picked up speed.

Under his helmet, he heard wind rush past his ears in a muffled moan, and he had to squint his eyes so they wouldn't tear. The white wall rushed toward him.

Fifteen meters.

Some slashers had a reputation for being lazy, unambitious delinquents. In Zak's case it wasn't true. You had to be brave and very ambitious to try a vertical ride. Even with the anticollision system, it took real courage to stay calm while you hurtled at high speed toward a solid wall.

Ten meters.

Zak kept his mind on his next move. The real trick to a vertical climb wasn't getting the nose up—the skimboard did most of the work for you. It was the moment afterward. Once the board banked, its nose was pointing straight up into the air. That meant the bottom-side repulsors were pushing off the wall. Unless the rider kept his balance perfectly, and cut power to the bottom repulsors at just the right moment, the board would push off the wall, flipping the rider over and dropping him straight into the ground.

Five meters.

Zak braced himself.

One meter.

Now!

Zak leaned back as the anticollision kicked in. The nose of the skimboard tilted up and Zak tilted with it. Suddenly he was looking up at the sky. Using the foot

71

controls, he transferred power from the bottom repulsors to the rear engine, trying to gain altitude.

But he forgot to compensate for the skimboard's newly improved engine. The same thrusters that had pushed him off the ground were now pushing him *away* from the wall. Zak and his board tipped over backward. He was no longer looking at the sky, he was looking at the town—which was upside down. Or rather, *he* was. Then gravity, aided by the power of his own upside-down repulsors, drove him right into the ground with a thud.

He was very glad that he had worn his helmet.

Even so, he felt like his brain had exploded inside his head. He lay flat on his back for a moment, staring at the sky. It felt as though his entire body had just become one big bruise, and he decided he couldn't possibly feel any worse.

Until his view of the sky was blocked by the blubbery body of Smada the Hutt.

"How convenient," Smada said. "We were just coming to kill you."

CHAPTER

Zak scrambled to his feet. But he was already surrounded by five Ganks. Smada the Hutt sat on his hoversled amid folds of fat flesh. The grinning slug stuck one hand into a large glass bowl filled with live eels. He dropped one of the wriggling eels into his mouth and licked his lips.

"Delicious. Now, where was I?" the Hutt rumbled. "Oh, yes. Boys."

The Ganks raised their weapons.

"Wait!" Zak cried. "Why are you doing this?"

"Blame your uncle," the crime lord said matter-of-factly. "He won't cooperate, so I've decided to *convince* him to work for me. I'm going to kidnap your sister, and kill you as a warning that I mean business."

"People will wake up soon, boss," one of the Ganks growled. "Lots of witnesses."

"You're right. Kill the boy and dump his body on the doorstep. Then we'll find the girl."

"Doomed!" Someone shrieked the word so loudly that even the Gank killers jumped back.

"Doomed!" the voice shrieked again.

Bebo appeared around a corner, shuffling through the center of town. He swayed this way and that and screamed at the top of his lungs. "We're all doomed!"

"That madman no longer amuses me," Smada bellowed. "Turn him into nerf meat."

One of the Ganks pointed his blaster at Bebo and fired. The blaster bolt streaked through the air straight toward Bebo. But then it missed. Zak blinked. He must have hit his head harder than he thought. He could have sworn that the blaster bolt veered away at the last minute.

"You missed!" one of the other Ganks laughed. "But I won't."

He fired one shot. Then a second. Both shots missed and shattered the side of a building far down the street. Bebo, shocked but unhurt, ran for cover.

All the Ganks lost their tempers. Five blasters fired at once, and the air was filled with the scream of energy bolts. Bebo was lost behind a cloud of dust and smoke.

When it cleared, Bebo lay cowering on the ground. But he was untouched.

74

"You cursed old fool!" Smada roared. "I'll kill you myself!"

"You'll kill no one, Smada." It was Hoole's voice.

Smada and his bodyguards turned. Behind them, Hoole stood at the head of two dozen villagers, foul-tempered from lack of sleep and all armed with blasters. Tash and Deevee stood behind the Shi'ido.

Smada laughed. He reached one fat hand into the bowl of eels and ate another one. "Hoole, you're a fool. Do you think a few frontier settlers are a match for my Ganks!"

Hoole's voice was like steel. "Do you want to kill that man so badly that you're willing to find out?"

"I am Smada the Hutt! I kill who I want, when I want."

"Not today."

Hoole waited.

A low, angry growl rumbled from deep within Smada's cavernous belly. He was a Hutt. That meant he wasn't afraid of a few villagers. But it also meant he was smart enough to know when to cut his losses. Winning this standoff wasn't worth the risk to his own precious skin.

"That's twice you've foiled me, Hoole," Smada said. "But in the end, you *will* work for me." The Hutt cast a threatening eye on Bebo. "And you'll be dead before another day is over."

One of the Ganks jumped on board the hoversled and

steered it down the street as the rest of the thugs followed. No one dared to stop them. Only when the crime lord was out of sight did the settlers, and Hoole, relax.

"Zak, are you all right?" Tash asked.

"I think so," her brother said. "I've got him to thank for it." He pointed at Bebo.

"Please," Bebo screeched to the gathered crowd. "You've got to listen to me. I've found something!"

But the settlers had had enough excitement for one morning. With a few short thanks from Hoole, they turned and headed back to their houses. "You're all doomed!" Bebo yelled after them.

"What happened?" Tash asked Zak.

Zak shrugged. "I don't know, but it saved my life. It was amazing. Those Ganks kept firing at him, but every single shot missed, and he just stood there. He's pretty brave."

"Or a fool," Deevee added.

"Um, Tash, I think you may have been right." Zak reddened a little. "At least about Smada's men being after us. He was after me this morning."

"I told you!" she nearly shouted.

"But I don't know anything about the Ganks *disappearing*," he added.

"Disappearing!" Bebo pounced on the word. "Yes, yes! Disappearing!"

Hoole interrupted. "Zak, Tash, please. It is too early in the day for this."

But Tash had finally found someone who believed her, even if he was a madman. "Uncle Hoole, I'd like to stay and talk with him for a while."

Hoole looked around. The Hutt was gone, but for how long? "I don't think that would be safe, Tash."

"Well then you can stay with me. Or Zak."

The Shi'ido shook his head. "I have to go," he said.

"Where?"

"I have more business to take care of," the Shi'ido said mysteriously. Again Tash was reminded of what Smada had told her the day before in the cantina. *What was Uncle Hoole up to?*

"And I didn't get much of a chance to practice my skimboarding," her brother explained.

"Just for a few minutes, Uncle Hoole. Please!" she pleaded.

Hoole relented. "Very well. Deevee will stay with you. I will meet you back at Chood's house. Do not go far."

"Prime," Tash muttered as her brother and uncle left. "The dreariest droid ever designed will make great company."

"I can't say I'm any happier than you are," Deevee intoned. "I'd rather be counting the sand fleas on a nerf. Although I could probably find plenty on your new friend here."

Bebo had squatted down in the dust. He rocked back and forth, muttering to himself. When Tash approached

77

him again and put a hand on his shoulder, he did not respond. "Bebo? That's your name, right?" No response. "Are you okay?" No response. "Do you know about these disappearances?"

"Disappearances!" The word brought Bebo to life. "Yes, the disappearances! You know."

"What can you tell me?"

"Let me show you what I found!" He leaped to his feet and grabbed Tash's hand. "Come on! Hurry!"

He rushed off, pulling Tash along behind him.

"This is beginning to look like an adventure," Deevee grumbled as he hurried after them. "I detest adventures."

Zak decided that his skimboard was a little too powerful. He walked back to the spaceport, where he could use the *Lightrunner*'s tools. He had watched Chewbacca work, and he was sure he knew what he was doing.

Using one of the *Lightrunner*'s landing pods as a seat, he popped open a panel on his skimboard. He would lower the power just enough so that he'd still have a powerful ride, but without as much height.

He was just about to make the adjustment when a shadow fell across him.

A moment later, Zak was gone.

———

Bebo led Tash away from the town and into the surrounding woods. It was a dark forest, where trees grew thick and very close together. Their trunks were gnarled, with big roots that broke out of the ground. They reminded Tash of tentacles.

"Um, should we really be out here?" she asked. She looked back, but Deevee had been left far behind.

Bebo didn't answer. Instead he led her even deeper into the forest, until they came to the base of an enormous tree. Giant roots curled up as high as Tash's head, and the branches were so thick that she could not see the sun. Beneath the tree, it was almost as dark as night. In the shadow of one of the great roots, Tash could just make out an opening in the ground.

"Down there," Bebo said, pointing toward the hole. "Go on."

"Down there?" she asked. "Are you sure it's safe?"

"Safe? Safe! Heh, heh, heh!" Bebo cackled. "If you wanted to be safe, you shouldn't have come to D'vouran!"

And he shoved her down the hole.

CHAPTER

Tash started to scream, but the fall was so short that her cry came out as a short "Yip!" as she landed on something as soft as a large cushion. Wherever she was, it was pitch black.

Tash had just enough sense to get out of the way before she heard Bebo drop down after her, still muttering and chuckling softly to himself.

"What are you doing! Why did you push me?" she yelled angrily.

"Sorry, sorry. Have to hurry, though. No time to waste."

She heard Bebo shuffle away into the darkness. "Don't leave me here! Where are you?"

But he didn't go far. Tash heard the creak of a lever being turned, and then light flooded the room.

She was standing in the middle of an underground laboratory. Or at least what used to be an underground laboratory. Vials and test tubes lay scattered on table-tops, and broken glass was everywhere. There was lots of computer equipment, too, but most of it was broken or taken apart.

Over in a corner, a dirty sleeping mat was unrolled, and bits and pieces of junk were gathered around it. Propped up on a little shelf, Tash noticed a few holographic pictures meant as keepsakes. All of them were of the same attractive woman. In the last holograph, the woman wore camping gear and looked like she'd been in the wild for months. In the background, Tash recognized the trees of D'vouran.

"Lonni," Bebo said.

"This is your friend Lonni?" Tash asked. "Then she does exist."

"Did exist. Did exist," Bebo mumbled. "Gone. Vanished." He heaved a long, sad sigh. "Come with me!"

Tash followed Bebo down a flight of stairs that led deeper underground. "We found the laboratory soon after the crash. The Imperials came after me. They wanted to arrest me."

"They blamed you for the crash," Tash said. "I read it on the HoloNet."

"They blamed me, but it wasn't my fault. D'vouran wasn't on the charts! It wasn't my fault!"

"I believe you," Tash said, although the truth was she wasn't sure what to believe.

In all the excitement, Tash seemed to have shaken the feeling that she was being watched. Though now, as she descended beneath the surface of D'vouran, the feeling came back stronger than ever. Whatever it was, she was drawing close to its source.

At the bottom of the stairs was a cavernous underground chamber, large enough to house a dozen star freighters. The steel walls were lined with more decrepit scientific equipment, and in the center of the room was a vast pit. It must have measured twenty meters across. It led down even deeper into the planet . . . so deep that Tash could not see the bottom. The hair on the back of her neck rose.

Whatever was in the pit was pure evil.

"What is this place?" she whispered.

Bebo whispered, too. "We only found the top chamber at first. I didn't uncover these stairs until recently. This place must have been here before we came."

There was a winch and a crane attached to the side of the pit. Obviously, at some point, things—maybe even people—must have been lowered into the pit by whoever ran the laboratory. Tash couldn't imagine who would have the courage to go down there. She peeked over the edge of the pit and shuddered. There was nothing there, but the feeling of overwhelming dread was so powerful, it made her dizzy. Yet, at the same time, it triggered something else inside her, a powerful and comforting force that seemed to fight against her fear and give her strength. But the feeling of terror grew stronger. Whatever was making people disappear, it had started here. She was sure of it.

"Maybe the Enzeen built it," she suggested.

"Maybe. But what's that?" Bebo pointed at markings on the wall. Tash gasped.

Carved into the wall was the insignia of the Empire, old and worn but unmistakable.

Everyone in the galaxy recognized that symbol. It looked like a wheel within a wheel—like a star inside a black circle. But everything about it was rigid and mechanical, as though declaring that even the stars obeyed the Emperor.

Tash was jolted by a sudden roar. Her heart stopped and she scurried away from the pit, thinking that whatever lay down there was coming up. Bebo squealed and cowered, covering his ears as a second roar echoed through the underground laboratory. Tash frantically looked around for the source of the terrible noise.

And saw Deevee standing at the bottom of the stairs.

"Deevee!" she cried. "Did you do that?"

The droid stepped between Tash and Bebo. "Don't worry, Tash. I am fully capable of protecting you."

"Protect me? From what?"

"From this madman," the droid said. He glared at Bebo, who still lay trembling on the floor, his hands covering his ears. "He tried to kidnap you. Luckily I am equipped with infrared sensors and was able to follow you through the forest."

Tash couldn't help but smile. This was a side of the droid that she'd never seen before. "Why D-V9, you actually came to my rescue!"

The droid seemed to straighten a little. "That is my job."

"I thought you hated taking care of us," Tash pointed out. "Maybe you decided we're not so bad after all, hmm?"

Deevee sniffed. "Nonsense. I just try to do a good job, whatever it is." He looked at Bebo. "I take it, then, that you are in no danger?"

"Not from him. What was that sound you made?"

Deevee pointed at his mouth—the tiny speaker on the front of his face. "Part of my job as a research unit is— was, I should say—to record sounds that I hear. Once, on a visit to the planet Tatooine, I heard a krayt dragon. I thought it might come in useful."

Tash coaxed Bebo out of his shock while Deevee examined the room. "This equipment is in poor shape," he observed, "but it is very complicated machinery. Whoever built this must have been working on a highly advanced experiment."

"What do you think they were doing?" Tash asked.

"I cannot say," the droid replied, examining an old computer terminal. "Most of the equipment is gone, and the computer files have been destroyed. But it was something important. Master Hoole will want to know about this immediately.''

Tash turned sharply. "He will? Why? Deevee, what is Uncle Hoole up to? Why did Smada the Hutt say there's a lot about our uncle that we don't know?''

"I could not tell you," Deevee replied quickly.

"Couldn't?'' Tash accused. "Or won't?''

Bebo piped up. "Don't argue! There's no time. Don't you see?''

"No, I do not,'' Deevee answered. "I see nothing but an old hermit, half out of his mind, who lives in an abandoned laboratory. And if people have been disappearing for so long, why haven't you gone with them?''

In answer Bebo removed a small pendant from around his neck. "Look! Look!'' he urged.

Taking the pendant, Tash saw that it was a tiny device encased in crystal.

"What is it?'' she asked.

"This,'' Bebo said, "is protection.''

"From what?'' Deevee asked.

"I don't know,'' the madman replied. "The technology is too advanced for me, but I think it makes some kind of energy field. I found it here in the laboratory and kept it to study later. Ever since then, I've been safe from whatever is causing people to disappear.''

Deevee was skeptical. "Which is what?''

"I wish I knew!" Bebo said.

"Then how do you know you're safe?" Deevee scoffed.

"Because I'm still here," Bebo rasped. "I have not disappeared. Others have. Many others."

Many others? Tash wondered. "What do you mean? Tell me what happened."

Bebo sighed. Finally he said, "D'vouran wasn't on the charts. We crashed. Twenty of us survived, including Lonni and me. We sent out a distress signal and waited. But we were fine. The Enzeen had welcomed us. They treated us well, and they fed us." His eyes grew distant. He was remembering something terrible. "Then people started disappearing. At first, just one or two. We thought they'd gotten lost in the forest. Then another, and another. Then in groups of two or three! They just disappeared!"

He shuddered in fright. "We didn't know what to do. We searched for them but never found a trace. Instead, the last few of us found this place. We stayed here. As long as we were here, no one disappeared. But we had to check the distress beacon. And every person who went out, never came back."

"What about the Enzeen?" Tash asked. "Couldn't they help?"

Bebo twitched. "I don't trust them." He continued. "Finally only Lonni and I were left. The Enzeen told us that the Empire had investigated the crash and blamed me. I had to hide here. It was the only safe place. Then when I heard that settlers were coming to D'vouran, I had to warn them. I had to tell them about the disappearing!"

His shoulders slumped. "But they won't listen. I didn't have any proof. Not until now."

Although they were alone, Bebo's voice had become a whisper.

Deevee examined the pendant. "There is some kind of circuit inside," the droid announced. "It appears to be a kind of tiny energy generator. I'd say it creates a small force field, like the starship shielding used to deflect blasters. But this one is much smaller. And it's been tuned to a very unusual frequency. I'm not sure what it's for. However, it does match the design of the equipment around us."

Tash concluded: "So whatever it is, this pendant was left by the same people who built this place. The Empire. Maybe Bebo's right, Deevee. Maybe people *are* disappearing. And I bet this laboratory has something to do with it. You're right, Deevee, we should tell Uncle Hoole."

Tash and Deevee wanted to return to the village, but Bebo wouldn't follow. "Stay here!" he pleaded. "It's not safe outside. That's how people vanish. That's how everyone goes. In here, it's safe."

"I'm sorry, Bebo. I have to go."

"Then take this." He put the pendant back into her hand. "It will protect you out there."

Tash tried to refuse. "I can't take it, Bebo. It's yours."

"Take it!" Bebo insisted. "They think I'm mad with guilt. Maybe they're right. But you believe me. So you must convince them. There is a danger!"

Tash slipped the pendant over her head and hid it under her shirt. "Thank you."

"We've been gone too long, Tash," Deevee urged. "I must report to Master Hoole."

Tash suddenly realized that Uncle Hoole and Zak were in danger. They were out there on the planet, without the protection of a device like the one Bebo had given her. They had to hurry. "Thanks, Bebo," Tash said to the man. "I still don't know what's going on here, but at least I do know there's a bigger mystery than Smada the Hutt."

Tash and Deevee climbed out of the laboratory and hurried through the shadows under the trees.

Back in the laboratory, Bebo huddled near the edge of the terrible pit. He was afraid of it, but he knew that somehow it was the cause of all the evil he had seen. Now, at last, someone else believed him.

There was a rumble from deep within the dark abyss.

The rumble became a groan.

Bebo leaned over the edge of the pit. For just a moment he thought he saw something moving down there.

But he did not see the Gank killer creep up behind him until it was too late.

"This is from Smada the Hutt," the Gank snarled, raising his blaster. "It's your turn to disappear." He fired. The bolt struck Bebo and sent him tumbling into the pit.

Halfway back to the village, Tash asked Deevee, "Do you think Uncle Hoole will believe me now?"

"I cannot say," the droid replied. "There is certainly a laboratory here, but what does that mean? It was abandoned long ago. If there is foul play about, I'd say it has far more to do with Smada the Hutt than with an abandoned laboratory. He is the real danger on this planet."

But Tash had stopped listening. Another sound had reached her ears.

Slurp-slurp.

The same sound she had heard last night. "Do you hear that?"

Slurp-slurp.

"Yes," the droid replied. "A most unusual sound. Not unlike the bloodsucking leeches of Circarpous Four—"

"It's coming from over there."

With Deevee close behind, Tash crept toward the sound.

Slurp-slurp. Slurp-slurp.

Not only did the sound grow louder, but it multiplied many times.

And it was coming from just beyond the next tree.

Tash cautiously pulled a branch out of the way and peered into a small clearing. At first she was relieved. All she saw were a few Enzeen standing around the clearing. As Tash watched, she saw another Enzeen step into the clearing. It was Chood.

Tash opened her mouth to call out to him. Then she gagged.

Chood opened his own grinning mouth and stuck out his tongue. It was surprisingly thick, and incredibly long, and wriggled out of his mouth like a long, thick snake. It squirmed in the air for a moment, then plunged deep into the ground.

Slurp-slurp.

Slurp-slurp.

The sucking sound filled the air.

What was Chood doing?

Tash pulled the tree branch even farther back to get a better look. But the branch snapped with a loud crack. The startled Enzeen looked right at her.

She saw Chood's face clearly. The friendly smile fell away, revealing a hate-filled glare. "She has seen us. Get her!"

The group of Enzeen started toward them. Tash was confused. Why were they angry?

"Run!" Deevee yelled, pulling Tash away from the clearing.

For the second time in two days, Tash was running for her life.

Tash and Deevee rushed away from the small clearing. But the Enzeen were much too fast. They came up quickly from behind, and Tash could see them slipping through the trees on either side. Soon they would be surrounded.

Beside her, Deevee's mechanical joints whined as he tried to keep up with his human companion. He was not designed for sprints through the woods. Tash leaped over a tree root. Behind her, Deevee tripped and fell clattering to the ground. The Enzeen were on him instantly. "Deevee!" Tash yelled, slowing down.

"Run!" the droid cried out. Then he was buried beneath a pile of Enzeen.

Tash heard them pounding mercilessly on his metal body. As she ran, she looked back over her shoulder, hoping to catch a glimpse of the droid.

When she looked forward again, an Enzeen was standing in front of her.

Tash dodged to the left. But there was another, and another. Everywhere she looked, there were Enzeen. She was surrounded.

She struggled, kicking and punching as the Enzeen grabbed hold of her. But there were too many of them. "What's going on?" she demanded. "Why are you making people disappear?"

One of the Enzeen laughed an evil laugh. "We have harmed no one."

"Then what's going on here?" Tash demanded.

The Enzeen laughed again. "You will never know."
He looked at his companions. "Chood will catch up in
a moment. We'll hold her until then."

Tash gave up struggling. The Enzeen were too strong
for her. She started to tremble as the feeling of dread
began to overwhelm her. And yet, as it had in the laboratory, her fear sparked another feeling, a sense of
peace and calm, powerful, like some kind of force.

The Force.

Tash had searched for it. Hoped for it. Longed for it.
But she never actually thought she had it. But she felt
something. Didn't she?

"You've got nothing to lose," she told herself.

Tash closed her eyes. She tried to call on the Force.
Taking a deep breath, she remembered what the Jedi
had written about the Force. *The Force surrounds us,*
she had read, *it binds us together. It can draw objects to
us, or push them away. It is the most powerful force in
all the galaxy. The strength of armies, of starfleets, even
the strength of planets, is nothing compared to the
power of the Force.*

Tash imagined the Force as a field of energy pushing
the Enzeen back. At first she felt foolish. But slowly her
embarrassment gave way to calm. She forgot about her
fear. A warm tingle spread through her body. She imagined the energy field expanding, driving the shrieking
creatures farther and farther away. As she did, the tingle
in her body grew into a strong electric current, running

from the top of her head down to her toes. For just an instant she felt a sense of connection with something larger than herself, larger even than the planet on which she stood.

That's when the ground began to move.

It started as a low rumble. The ground started to tremble beneath their feet. In seconds the rumble became a roar, and the trembling turned into a full-fledged groundquake. The Enzeen shouted in surprise. Trees started to creak, and a few of them snapped and crashed to the ground. Tash was thrown off her feet, coughing as the groundquake kicked up clouds of dust and dried leaves. The sun seemed to vanish as the sky grew dark. Somewhere in the distance Tash heard the loudest sound she would ever hear, a sound like two mountains grinding together. The grinding, booming explosion seemed to come from above and below. Later, thinking back, Tash imagined that if a planet could speak, it would speak in a voice that loud.

The quake ended even faster than it had begun. There was a final boom, like a giant door closing, and then the terrible noise just stopped. Tree branches, shaken by the quake, continued to vibrate for a few seconds. Then there was silence. Only the gloom remained. The day seemed to have gone from midmorning to late afternoon in a few seconds. It was as though the groundquake had caused the planet to spin closer toward night.

Did I do that? she wondered in awe.

The groundquake had surprised the Enzeen as much as it surprised Tash. They, too, had fallen to the ground. Tash saw her chance.

She ran.

This time she didn't look back. She ran as fast as she could, ignoring the branches and twigs that scratched her. If she could just reach the village, Hoole and the settlers would help her.

Tash did not hear anyone following her. The Enzeen had been too startled by the tremors to chase her. She knew that wouldn't last, so she kept running. She wouldn't stop until she was safe.

She saw the buildings of the village through the trees. Her heart leaped! She was going to make it! She was going to be safe!

Tash broke through the trees into the village, shouting, "Uncle Hoole, Uncle Hoole! Zak! Anybody!"

No one answered.

She shouted it again and again, running from door to door. She ran down the main street. She ran to the spaceport. She ran to the Don't Go Inn.

But the village was completely deserted.

CHAPTER 13

She was all alone.

Somehow every person in the village had vanished. Uncle Hoole was gone. Zak was gone. Even Deevee was gone. Tash's worst nightmare had come true. She had been abandoned.

She knew the Enzeen would find her soon. She didn't care. Her entire family was gone. Her poor parents had been vaporized in the destruction of Alderaan. Now Hoole and Zak had vanished, along with a village full of settlers.

Then an even more terrible thought struck her.

Had she caused it?

She had tried to call on the Force. Instead a groundquake had erupted. Had the groundquake swallowed the villagers—and Hoole and Zak? And had she created the groundquake with the Force?

The thought pressed down upon her like the weight of a planet.

Weak and defeated, Tash walked to the spaceport. All the ships were still there. No one had *flown* off the planet. But they were still gone.

Tash stopped in front of the *Lightrunner*. Briefly she considered trying to fly it away, to escape from the Enzeen. But she knew she couldn't do it. She could only pretend to be a pilot. She couldn't really fly a starship.

Dragging her feet, Tash stubbed her toe on something. It was a flat board about a meter and a half long, with stick-strips across the top and thruster vents on the back.

Zak's skimboard.

What was it doing here?

Next to it, Tash noticed a shattered glass bowl . . . and amid the broken glass were three or four small, slimy bodies. Eels. A bowl full of eels.

Smada the Hutt had been there. And so had Zak.

Tash tried to steady her beating heart. Maybe Zak hadn't vanished. Maybe he had been kidnapped by Smada. Maybe Zak was right. Smada was behind all the disappearances.

But then what about the Enzeen? What were they? And why had they wanted to kill her?

Tash felt questions ricochet around in her head like blaster bolts. She didn't know the answers. She only knew one thing, and that was that it appeared that her brother had been captured by Smada.

Which meant he might still be alive.

Tash tucked the skimboard under her arm and left the spaceport. She headed through the village looking for Smada's stronghold.

She did not notice something creeping slowly behind her.

Smada's stronghold was not difficult to find. As her uncle had told her, it lay just inside the forest on the far side of the village. Two towers of ugly brown stone rose up out of the trees. From a distance they looked like misshapen giants. By Hutt standards it was a small place, more like a summer cabin than a fortress, but to Tash it looked like a mansion.

It was nearly dark by the time Tash arrived there. Again she wondered what had happened to the day. Was it just later than she thought? But, no, she had only been awake for a few hours. Yet the day was all but gone.

She walked right up to the front door and knocked.

The Ganks let her in. They searched her thoroughly and made her leave the skimboard beside the door. Beyond the door was a large audience hall, just big enough to fit a Hutt's ego. There were six Gank bodyguards in the room. Smada the Hutt lolled atop his hoversled, chuckling to himself. In one corner, in a small cage, sat her brother.

"Tash!" he called out.

"Welcome," Smada said. "I've been expecting you."

"Let my brother go," Tash demanded.

The Ganks laughed.

"Certainly," Smada said. "As soon as you tell me where Hoole is."

Tash was stunned. "I don't know where he is. I thought *you* had captured him."

"Me?" the Hutt replied. "Don't be a fool, girl. If I had your uncle already, I wouldn't bother with you and your brother. You two are meaningless, but Hoole's Shi'ido powers will make me millions!"

"Your millions won't mean anything if you're dead," she said defiantly. "Do you have any idea what's going on around here? Didn't you feel the groundquake?"

Smada shrugged. "A tremor. Nothing significant."

"Have you been to the village? Everyone's gone!"

Smada sniffed. "As I said, nothing significant. Those villagers don't concern me. I wouldn't care if the ground opened up and swallowed them all. As long as I get my Shi'ido."

Tash tried again to convince him. "You're in as much danger as we are, Smada. People are disappearing. And the Enzeen are evil. They tried to kill me."

Smada laughed. "*I* will kill you, if you don't tell me where your uncle is. No, wait, I have a better idea."

He motioned to one of his Gank bodyguards. The enormous Gank plucked Zak out of his cage and dragged him to Smada's hoversled. "Let go of me, you ugly—"

"Silence," Smada growled threateningly. Zak glared at him but said nothing.

Pointing his blaster at Zak, Smada turned to Tash. "Tell me where your uncle is, or I will kill your brother."

CHAPTER

Tash didn't know what to say. How could she save Zak when she didn't know the answer to Smada's question?

But she had to say something.

Tash opened her mouth to speak. And as she did an enormous roar blasted through the chamber, echoing off the walls and deafening them all. Smada dropped his blaster and tried to cover his ears with his flabby hands. Even the ruthless Ganks shrieked and covered their ears. It was like nothing they had ever heard.

Except Tash, who recognized it.

It was the sound of a krayt dragon roaring.

Deevee stood in the doorway. He was battered and dented, but he was functioning. "Catch!" he called out, and slid something toward them.

It was Zak's skimboard. It clattered along the floor

until Tash stopped it with one foot. "Zak, come on!" She stepped on board and felt the stick-strips cling to her feet. Zak was still a little disoriented, but he managed to hop on board as well. "Brace yourself," he warned.

He activated the repulsors, and Tash felt her stomach drop out. They were suddenly floating three meters in the air. "C-can't you fly any lower?"

Zak actually laughed. "Nope. This is the *lowest* setting."

"Get them!" Smada roared. The Hutt and his bodyguards had recovered quickly from the shock of the dragon roar, but they were startled again to see their two prisoners suddenly floating so high off the ground.

"Blast them!"

The Ganks opened fire.

Zak and Tash saw white-hot energy beams flash around them. They heard blaster fire sizzle the air, and they smelled the acrid odor of ion burn.

But not a single shot touched them. "These guys are lousy shots!" Zak laughed.

Tash remembered the gangsters' attack on Bebo. "It's not them, Zak. It's this!" She pulled out the pendant she still wore. "This is what Bebo was wearing. It protected him from disappearing. And I think it protected him from the blasters!"

But there was no time to examine the device. The blaster bolts were missing them, but they came awfully close. Zak kicked the skimboard into gear and slashed toward the exit, where Deevee waited. Some of the Ganks continued to fire, while others leaped up, trying to grab them out of the sky. Zak twisted and turned the skimboard to dodge them.

"We have to get Deevee!" Tash said. "Are you sure this thing will lift all three of us?" she asked.

"Are you kidding?" Zak replied. "The way it's supercharged, it could carry a Hutt! But there isn't *room* for three people on board."

Tash yelled down to Deevee. "Grab hold of the bottom!"

Now that they were closer, Tash could see how badly damaged the droid was. Wiring was exposed where his silver covering had been torn away. Every inch of his body had been dented.

With a tremendous leap, the damaged droid launched himself upward and grabbed hold of the skimboard. He was hanging on the underside of the hoverboard, and the repulsors blasted him, but he held on.

"Can you make it, Deevee?" Tash called out.

"I don't seem to have much choice!" the droid replied. "Go!"

Zak hit the accelerator, and they zoomed out the open door. They were going to escape!

"You're all useless fools!" Smada the Hutt snarled at his Gank bodyguards.

He had not become a crime lord through ruthlessness

alone—he had a brilliant and devious mind. He knew it was impossible that all his Gank bodyguards were missing their targets.

Smada picked up his blaster and took careful aim at the receding skimboard. He squeezed the trigger twice.

The high-velocity energy bolts covered the distance in an eye-blink. The first shot passed right over Deevee's head and between his arms. The second shot creased the skimboard's underside, cutting off the propulsion that kept the board aloft. The microengines whined once, then the skimboard bucked wildly and dropped.

"Look out!" Tash cried. The hoverboard disappeared from beneath her feet and she was falling through the darkness. The ground rushed up to meet her and she struck it hard.

The wind had been knocked out of her, and she gasped. Next to her, she heard Zak suddenly shriek, "Help! Help!" Instinctively she grabbed for him and touched his arm. Instantly his shrieking stopped.

"What's wrong?" she yelled.

"I-I don't know," her brother said in utter confusion. "I felt something grab me. Then when you touched me, it stopped."

"Did you see it?"

"Tash, I can barely see you! It's pitch black out here."

It was true. Night had fallen. Which was impossible . . . unless the planet had begun to spin faster in space.

Tash stood up, and immediately Zak screamed again. Tash felt his hand clutch desperately at her. "Don't let go! Don't let go of me again!" he whimpered.

The fear in his voice terrified her. "What is it?"

Zak the daredevil, Zak the risktaker, was trembling with fright. "I don't know. I don't want to know. But it's strong. And it will get me if you let go!"

CHAPTER

"Deevee, can you see anything?" Tash asked. "Use your infrared."

"It's not functioning," the droid replied. "Most of my systems are off-line, thanks to that beating the Enzeen gave me. Thank goodness they left me for scrap before the job was done!"

"The Enzeen?" Zak asked, bewildered. "They attacked you?"

Tash quickly told her brother about the laboratory. The groundquake. The empty village. And that Hoole was missing.

Zak's voice was trembling as he said, "Great. What do we do? Smada's behind us somewhere. The

Enzeen are trying to kill you. Uncle Hoole's gone. And there's something in this darkness that's after us!"

"Is the skimboard working?" Tash asked.

Deevee had a tiny glowrod hooked into his photoreceptors, still functioning, which he lit for Zak. In the small beam of light, Zak examined his board. A long black scar ran across the board's main repulsor vent. The sharp smell of ozone lingered where Smada's shot had struck. "It's not going anywhere now. The microalluvial damper's shot. But I think I can fix it if I get a minute to rewire it."

"We'd better make a run for it then. Deevee, can you run?"

"No," the droid said matter-of-factly. "You'll have to leave me behind."

"Not this time," Tash said. She put one arm around his waist. Zak assumed a similar position on the droid's other side.

"Which way?" Zak asked.

"Toward the spaceport. Maybe together we can fly the *Lightrunner* out of here."

"I think not." A bright beam of light fell across them. Smada and his men had found them already.

The Hutt sat atop his hoversled, with his six Ganks around him. He glared at Zak and Tash through narrow slits. "Bring them here."

One of the Ganks lunged forward to grab them.

Then he vanished.

"Aiiiiiieeeeee!" A piercing scream sliced the air. "Help! Help me! It's got me! *Aiiiieee—!"* It was suddenly cut off.

Smada shined his searchlight onto the spot where the thug had been. But there was nothing there.

Not even a footprint.

"What is it?" Deevee cried. "What's going on?"

Out of the darkness, Smada answered. His voice was still powerful and commanding, but there was fear in it as well. "Something is out there." He shouted to his guards. "Bring those brats to me and let's get out of here!"

Cautiously another Gank stepped forward, while the others kept their blasters ready. This time Smada kept the searchlight trained on his henchman's back.

And this time they saw it. In the blink of an eye, a hole opened right under his feet and he dropped down. "Help!" the thug screamed.

The Gank threw his arms out wide as he was sucked downward, stopping his fall at his shoulders. He tried to scramble out of the hole, but it snapped shut around him like a jaw closing tight. The ground itself squeezed around his chest and he grunted in pain.

By that time the other Ganks had reached him. They grabbed hold of his hands and arms and tried to pull him out of the hole. But instead something far, far stronger pulled him another inch into the ground.

108

"Aaiiiiii!" the Gank screamed. It was terrifying to hear that sound come from the battle-scarred thug. "It's hurting me! It's hurting me!" His eyes were alive with terror. "I'm being eaten alive!"

Tash and Zak looked on, frozen with terror. "Blast it!" Smada roared.

"Blast what?" his guards shouted back. "There is nothing!"

They watched helplessly as the Gank's head was drawn in, and then the rest of his body, until all that remained was one hand sticking up out of the dirt. Finally the hand, too, disappeared. The hole closed up as if it had never been, and the victim was gone.

For the rest of the bodyguards, it was the last straw. Smada didn't pay them enough for this. They searched for someplace safe. But what place was safe from the ground itself?

Smada's hoversled.

The five remaining Ganks swarmed the floating platform, trying to escape the creature beneath the ground. There wasn't enough room on the crowded sled, and they began to scratch and claw one another like men fighting over the last life pod in a doomed starship.

"Get back, you spice-grubbing muckworms!" the Hutt commanded. He swung his thick tail, sweeping them off his sled.

All but one of the Ganks were dragged screaming into the ground. Each time the hole sealed up as if it had never been. In moments, Smada's henchmen had vanished.

Zak, Tash, and Deevee stood on the ground. The monster seemed uninterested in Deevee. Tash was protected, and Zak was too, as long as he held her hand. Atop the hoversled sat the surviving Gank killer and Smada the Hutt. Smada's massive frame shook with anger.

"WHAT IS THIS!" The roar exploded out of Smada the Hutt like a thunderclap. The mighty Hutt rose up to his full height, balancing himself on the tip of his thick body. Stretched out, Smada stood three meters above the deck of his hoversled, dwarfing even his Gank guard. It was an awesome sight to behold, and his voice boomed powerfully enough to conjure a demon.

Instead it conjured the Enzeen.

They melted out of the forest, twenty of them, all carrying lamps. They walked calmly across the ground, unafraid of whatever it was that had just swallowed up five Ganks.

Tash recognized the lead Enzeen.

"*Chood.*" Smada's voice was like a dagger. "What is going on here!"

Chood returned Smada's smoldering glare with a look of bored disdain. "Your doom."

"Bah!" Smada curled back to his usual prone position. "This is some trick of yours. There is a beast, a

110

creature that tunnels under the ground and hides. It attacks from below."

Chood smiled. "The beast does not hide."

Next to Smada, the Gank pounded his fist on the hoversled deck. "Then where *is* the beast? Where!"

All the Enzeen chuckled. As it had before, Chood's smile became evil. "After all this time you still do not understand! The secret of D'vouran has escaped you." He laughed a low, cruel laugh. "You think you will be eaten by a creature beneath the planet. You do not realize that you will be eaten by the planet itself!"

CHAPTER

Chood roared with laughter.

Tash shuddered. The planet. It was the planet. That was the source of her feeling of dread. That was why she felt like she was being watched. The planet—everything around her—was watching.

She looked down at the ground and wondered what waited beneath: invisible teeth tearing the flesh from their bones. The strength seemed to melt out of her legs, and she clung to Zak for support.

But Zak was just as scared. The ground, the simple, solid ground they walked on every minute of every day, had suddenly become a monster. And the only thing protecting them was a tiny pendant hanging around Tash's neck.

In the midst of all this terror, Smada the Hutt picked

a speck of dirt from his fingernail. He had already forgotten about his henchmen. They could be replaced. His devious mind had already bent around the terror of his situation, and he moved on in search of ways to exploit it. He was a Hutt after all.

"Chood," he began carefully. "I'm sure we can come to some sort of arrangement. Perhaps if I were to offer you, say, two million credits to assure my safe passage?"

"I wouldn't offer you safe passage even if I could," the Enzeen replied. "We don't control D'vouran. It feeds when it wants to. And it hungers."

Smada didn't miss a beat. "It can have the children."

"Thanks a lot, you ugly slug!" Zak yelled.

"Quiet, boy!" The bark crept back into Smada's voice. "We are bargaining here."

Chood shook his head. "There will be no bargain. D'vouran's hunger will be sated."

"Then why doesn't it eat you?" Tash wondered.

The Enzeen burst into coarse laughter. A few of them stomped their feet on the ground. Chood said, "We live in harmony with the planet. We make sure the planet is fed, and in return, the planet feeds us."

"*Feeds* you?" Zak asked. "How?"

In answer Chood opened his mouth wide. Again the wriggling tongue came out and plunged into the surface of D'vouran. Several of the other Enzeen did the same. The *slurp-slurp* of their feeding filled the air.

"I'm going to be sick," Zak moaned.

Deevee was the first to understand what he saw. "Since this planet is alive, the Enzeen must somehow suck nutrients from the ground."

"They're parasites," Tash whispered.

Chood's tongue detached itself from the ground and disappeared back into his mouth. He licked his lips and smiled. "D'vouran allows us to live on its body because we attract food. As long as it remains fed, we continue to feed off of it."

"You *lure* people here to be eaten?" Zak repeated incredulously.

Chood smiled. "Our goal is to serve." He laughed.

Tash shivered. But she couldn't help asking, "But why didn't it just swallow us whole when we first arrived?"

Chood looked at her as though she was a fool. "What purpose would that serve? D'vouran eats one meal a day, or two, but any more and it would frighten other victims away. Instead D'vouran takes its meals slowly. It toyed with you, taking a victim here, a morsel there."

"Until it took the whole town!" Tash cried.

The Enzeen jabbed a finger at Tash. "And that is your fault!"

Tash cringed. "My fault? How?"

"You and that meddling madman began to discover D'vouran's secret. The planet could not risk your escape, so it consumed everyone in the town the minute they stepped out of their houses during the ground-quake.''

"Then why doesn't it eat Hoole's brats?'' Smada asked.

Chood blinked. He had only just realized that, while Smada sat atop his hoversled, Zak and Tash were standing with their feet on the ground. The Enzeen moved in.

"Keep away!'' Deevee warned. He grabbed hold of one of the Enzeen, but another reached behind him and found a tiny switch on the droid's back. D-V9 was deactivated and fell to the ground. "Deevee!'' Tash cried.

Chood pointed to the skimboard strapped to Zak's back. "You there!'' he said to another Enzeen. "Remove that device.''

Tash's heart stopped when Chood's eyes found the pendant around her neck.

To her surprise, he did not pull it off. "Interesting. You have been to the laboratory. I should have known something like this might have been left behind by the creators.''

"Creators?'' she asked. "Did someone *make* this planet?''

Chood was just about to pluck the pendant from her neck, sending her into oblivion, but his eye glinted suddenly. "I think I'll answer your question. Take them!''

The Enzeen moved with frightening speed. Zak and Deevee were dragged down beside Tash, and a heavy fiber net was cast over them. They struggled for a moment, but a threatening growl from the Enzeen quieted them down.

The rest of the Enzeen closed in on the hoversled. Smada's Gank guard panicked and jumped from the sled, dashing through the trees. The Enzeen did not bother to chase him. They covered Smada in a net far larger and tougher than the one holding Tash, Zak, and Deevee.

The Gank had hardly run a dozen meters before he cried out and stumbled. His foot had caught on a hole in the ground. But when the killer tried to pull his foot loose, he found that the hole had closed up around his ankle. The Gank tried to kick himself loose of the planet. Instead some enormous force grabbed hold of his leg and pulled him down.

Chood laughed again. "You see? There is no escape from D'vouran. There is nowhere to run."

While most of the warriors stood guard over their captives, a few of the Enzeen vanished into the woods. They quickly reappeared, carrying two long, stout poles. Still tangled in their net, Zak, Tash, and Deevee were bundled up and lashed to one of the poles, where they hung like a sack of blumfruit. Smada was similarly lashed to the other, but not without a fight.

"Bloodworms! Bantha fodder! I'll tear your eyes out and eat your brains! Hutts will leave their slime tracks on your forgotten graves!"

He fought against the webbing that bound him, but

116

the Enzeen nimbly avoided his clutching arms and thrashing tail. Two or three Enzeen stationed themselves at the ends of each pole, then lifted the carrying bars onto their shoulders.

Only when the humans were securely bound and their feet no longer touched the planet did Chood grab the pendant. With a yank, he pulled it from around her neck.

"Chood!" Tash pleaded. "What are you going to do?"

Chood hissed with undisguised glee. "I am going to give you the answer to your question. I am going to take you to the Heart of D'vouran. There you will meet a death that makes these other deaths seem like a gift. In the Heart of D'vouran, every last nutrient from your body can be carefully digested. You will be eaten very slowly. Eaten alive."

CHAPTER

The Enzeen took them to the underground laboratory.

There, in the deep chamber, Zak, Tash, and Smada were brought to the edge of the pit. Tash thought she was as miserable as could be. Deevee's lifeless droid body was dumped next to her.

Terror seemed to flow from the pit like poisoned water from a fountain. Fear filled Zak and Tash. They were underground—*inside* a living creature, a terrible creature. And they were about to be fed to it.

"This is where your curiousity has gotten you," Chood declared. "You are about to enter a whole new world of pain. If you thought your friends and allies on the surface suffered, you were wrong. Their deaths were quick and merciful—most of them suffocated when they were pulled under D'vouran's surface. Here, in the Heart of D'vouran, the agony is a thousand times slower, and a thousand times worse, as the planet's victims are carefully digested week after painful week. Put them in!''

The Enzeen freed Zak and Tash from their net and shoved them onto the waiting platform. "Wait!" Chood ordered. He pointed to one of the Enzeen. "You! I thought I told you to remove that device!"

One of the Enzeen had forgotten to take away Zak's hoverboard. Under Chood's angry glare, he hurriedly detached the board from Zak's back, then stepped away.

It took four Enzeen to drag Smada onto the platform. They quickly freed him from his net as the platform was quickly shoved out over the pit. The massive Hutt thrashed about, roaring, "Bantha fodder! Nerf dung!"

The platform tilted crazily, and Zak and Tash clung to the support cables.

Chood addressed them from the edge of the pit, pointing down into the pit. "You wanted to know the secret of D'vouran. It lies here. From this place, D'vouran was first brought to life by its creators, and first learned to feed from this pit."

"Imperial scientists," Tash breathed. "They're always looking for new ways to hurt people."

Chood continued. "But the planet outgrew its creators and learned new and better ways to feed. The sci-

119

entists lost control of their creation. They were eaten like all who came after them. Now you will follow them.''

"Chood! Chood!" Smada bellowed. ''It's not too late! Four million credits! I will buy you a new planet!''

The Enzeen ignored him. Several of the blue-skinned creatures pushed the crane's arm, and the parasites began lowering the rope.

"We've got to do something!" Zak yelled.

"This is my fault." Tash said. Her throat was dry. Her voice was hardly a whisper. ''I should have listened to my feelings and made Uncle Hoole leave the planet. Then he'd be alive and we'd be safe!''

"It's not your fault, Tash," Zak said. ''I didn't listen to you. No one did.''

Tash peered down into the pit. Something at the bottom was writhing. And it was getting higher. As they were lowered into the pit, the writhing, throbbing mass rose up to meet them.

Tash couldn't watch. She looked up, into the faces of the Enzeen who ringed the pit. The more D'vouran ate, the more they could feed. All of them watched hungrily.

All of them but one.

The Enzeen who had taken the skimboard turned to Chood. Without warning, he raised the skimboard as high as he could, then brought it crashing down on Chood's head!

Chood crumpled to the ground. Instantly the Enzeen

120

pounced on him, tearing something small and shimmering from Chood's hand.

The pendant.

The other Enzeen charged. But the pendant-holder did something completely unexpected.

He changed shape. The parasites found themselves confronted not by one of their own but by a snarling Wookiee.

"Uncle Hoole!" Tash and Zak cried at once.

"Hoole!" boomed Smada. "Get us out of here!"

The Enzeen hesitated for only a moment. Then they swarmed the Wookiee, pounding him from every direction. The Wookiee fought back with powerful blows from one hand while he held the pendant high with the other.

And all the while, the platform continued to descend.

One of the Enzeen was thrown over the side of the pit. Zak and Tash watched as he fell, screaming, into the writhing molten mass below. In moments, all the Enzeen had been tossed aside.

With a few long strides, the Wookiee reached the crane. But before he could reverse its direction, something hard and heavy struck him from behind, slamming him against the crane. The crane's instruments snapped under the Wookiee's weight, and the platform stopped. The blow also broke Hoole's concentration, and he suddenly reverted back to his own Shi'ido shape as he fell to the ground.

Chood stood over Hoole, holding a thick metal pipe. "Give me that pendant!" He grabbed Hoole, trying to pry the crystal from the Shi'ido's fingers. They struggled right on the edge of the pit. Hoole was too groggy to resist, and in moments the pendant had changed hands again.

But just as he stood up, Chood lost his footing. He slipped and fell into the pit of D'vouran.

Taking the pendant with him.

Chood and the pendant vanished into the rising lava, and a moment later the molten mass shuddered and heaved.

"Pull us up!" Tash yelled. "Uncle Hoole! Pull us up!"

Hoole staggered toward the crane. But it wouldn't budge. "The crane is damaged! I can't move it!"

Beneath them, Tash could see the lava rising faster and faster. Great globs of molten planet leaped and sputtered toward them. D'vouran looked angry.

"We'd better think of something," she said, "or we're all going to die!"

CHAPTER 18

It was Zak who came up with the answer. "My skimboard!" he called up. "Do you still have my skimboard?"

Hoole picked it up. "Here! But it's not working."

"I can fix it! Toss it down!"

Hoole was as steady now as when the *Lightrunner* was out of control. He carefully measured the distance, and then tossed the hoverboard out and down into the pit.

Zak, Tash, and Smada all watched it spin through the air toward them. For a moment Tash thought it was going to miss them. But it landed dead in the middle of the platform as all three prisoners grabbed it.

"Got it!" Zak said. "Just give me a minute."

Tash looked down. "We don't have a minute!

Hurry!" The molten ground was only few meters below them, and it was rising fast.

"I think I've got it," Zak said, working frantically. "I've got it!"

The skimboard hummed to life. Zak jumped aboard and tested the ride. "It works!"

Zak, on the skimboard, hovered a few meters over the rising lava. He held his hand out to Tash, who took it and hopped quickly onto the board. She looked at the massive Hutt beside her. "But how are you going to fit him on here?"

"That is not a problem," Smada rumbled, "since I intend to leave you behind. Give me that board!"

The Hutt reached out to grabbed at Zak, but Zak slashed away and hovered a few meters off. "Don't be selfish! We can all make it if we work together!"

"No, no!" Smada howled. "I must have that device! It's mine!" with surprising agility, the Hutt lunged through the air. His fat fingertips grasped the edge of the skimboard, which tilted to one side, almost throwing Zak and Tash off.

The enormous Hutt's weight was too much for the hot-wired board. It began to sink quickly, like an overcrowded lifeboat taking on water.

"You're going to kill us all!" Tash yelled.

"Get back on the platform!" Zak pleaded. "We'll get off and we'll find a way to pull you up.

"Do you take me for a fool?" Smada snorted. "Let . . . me . . . on!"

But the skimboard had dropped almost to the molten surface. A weird tentacle of liquid mud reached up and wrapped itself around Smada's body, and the crime lord roared in pain and let go of the skimboard. The Hutt was sucked down into the molten mud of D'vouran.

As the Hutt fell, the skimboard, freed of his weight, rose upward.

But not high enough. The top of the pit was still six meters above them.

"Take us higher!" Tash said. "Get us out of here!"

"I can't," Zak said. "I'm at full power. The skimboard won't hover any higher than this."

"What do we do now?"

Zak looked at the wall of the pit. "I'll tell you what we're going to do," he said. "We're going to pull a vertical ride. And we're going to set a record."

Zak pressed the accelerator and guided the skimboard smoothly toward one end of the pit. He honestly didn't know if he could do it. He had blown his run yesterday morning, and that had only been five meters. Now he was going for six. A record.

Plus he was carrying a passenger. No one had ever pulled a vertical climb carrying passengers before. This really would be a record.

125

If he made it.

Zak took a deep breath. He would only get one chance. If he failed, he and his sister would be pitched backward, right into the Heart of D'vouran.

Zak gritted his teeth. "Hang on tight."

He bent into a crouch and kicked the skimboard into high gear. It slid rapidly toward the wall.

Ten meters. Seven meters. Five. Three. Now!

Anticollision buffers kicked in, bouncing the board's nose up into the air. Zak jammed all power from the bottom vents to the rear drive and leaned straight up, reaching for the ceiling high above. He felt the board shudder beneath his feet.

The engine whined. They weren't going to make it, he thought. It was a good try. It was the best ride of his life, but the pit was just too . . .

Then he was rocketing out of the pit, straight as a blaster bolt, up into the laboratory with Tash still on board.

"Yeeeahhhhh!"

Zak leaned forward, tipping the nose so that the bottom of the board was pointing down. The skimboard dropped until it reached its hovering altitude.

"Zak, you did it!" his sister cried.

"This is no time for celebration," Hoole warned.

Inside the pit, the churning grew more violent. Mud that looked like molten lava leaped up from the edges, grasping for prey. Zak and Tash pressed themselves against the walls of the laboratory.

"What's happening?" Zak yelled.

"It's the pendant!" Hoole replied. "It created an energy field D'vouran didn't like. That's why it wouldn't eat whoever was in contact with it. Now it's swallowed the energy field whole!"

Hoole ran to the corner where Deevee had been dumped and quickly reactivated the droid. D-V9 staggered to his feet. "Up the stairs!" Hoole commanded.

They ran for the stairs—Hoole and Tash helping Deevee along—that led up to the next level.

Just in time. The mud spilled over the edge of the pit, coating the floor in violent, shuddering slime. And it continued to rise.

They reached the exit. Only a few hours ago, Bebo had pushed Tash down that same hole.

"Zak," Hoole said. "Is this device powerful enough to carry you three back to the spaceport?"

"I think so."

"But we're not leaving you behind, Master Hoole!" Deevee insisted.

"Of course not," the Shi'ido replied.

Then Hoole vanished. For a moment they thought he was truly gone. Then Tash nearly jumped as a tiny white rodent jumped onto her leg and scampered up to her shoulder.

"Let's go!" she said.

The mud had crept up the stairs behind them. It was rising through the upper room now. It was chasing them.

Zak, Tash, and Deevee all crowded onto the skimboard. They barely fit, but when Zak hit the thrusters, it still lifted off the ground.

As quickly as he could, Zak guided the skimboard up and out of the laboratory. They rose up and out of the hole.

And into a nightmare.

All around them, as far as the eye could see, the ground had begun to boil. Trees sank into a boiling lava swamp. Balls of liquid dirt rose up and burst angrily around them. Snakelike strands of mud reached up to block their escape.

Zak pushed the skimboard along as fast as he dared, afraid that they would lose their balance and fall into D'vouran's waiting mass.

They passed over the town. Only the tops of the houses were visible. The rest had been sucked down into the muck.

"The spaceport's still standing!" Deevee said.

They could see the walls of the landing port, half sunk in mud. The top was still clear.

The skimboard flew through the spaceport gates and up the stairs. The minute the launchpad's tarmac was underneath them, Hoole leaped from Tash's shoulder, transforming in midair. He hit the ground running. "There's no time to lose!" he cried.

"Look!" Tash cried.

Large cracks opened up in the thick blast walls, and bubbling liquid earth began to ooze onto the tarmac.

"Get to the ship!" Hoole ordered.

The ooze wrapped itself around the landing gear of the other ships. As they scrambled into the *Lightrunner,* the mud was already reaching toward them.

CHAPTER

By the time Tash got to the cockpit, Hoole had already completed the ignition sequence and was ready to lift off. Zak and Tash strapped themselves in.

Hoole powered up the repulsor lift. The thrusters fired—but the ship didn't move.

Pressing her face against the transparent viewport, Tash looked down at the launchpad floor. The tarmac had completely vanished under D'vouran's mud. The living sludge rose waist-high all through the spaceport. The *Lightrunner* was caught in its unbreakable grip.

"We're trapped!" Deevee cried.

"I don't think my skimboard's going to help us this time," said Zak.

"It won't have to," Tash said. "Look up there!"

In the sky above the spaceport, a saucer-shaped ship

appeared. It dove toward them with surprising agility for a battered old Corellian freighter. Its pilot guided the ship over the *Lightrunner,* then skillfully powered down his repulsors until the freighter hovered only a few meters above the *Lightrunner.* It was a risky maneuver for most pilots.

But most pilots weren't Han Solo.

Zak and Tash popped open the top hatch of the *Lightrunner.* The noise from the underside of the *Millennium Falcon* was deafening, but it was a welcome sound to them, followed by the even more welcome sight of the *Falcon*'s belly-hatch opening wide. The face of Chewbacca the Wookiee poked through, roaring for them to hurry.

The boiling mud was halfway up the sides of the *Lightrunner.*

While Hoole pushed from below, Zak and Tash pulled Deevee up. Then they carried him over to the *Falcon*'s underside hatch. The Wookiee grabbed Deevee with one massive paw and easily hauled him up. Zak and Tash were next. Chewbacca picked them up as if they were rag dolls and brought them aboard Han Solo's ship, where he handed them off to the waiting arms of Luke Skywalker.

Han Solo's voice crackled over the comm system. "Come on, come on, what's taking so long down there?"

131

As soon as everyone was aboard, Luke signaled, "Everyone's accounted for, Han. Now get us out of here!"

The *Falcon* roared into motion.

Zak, Tash, and Hoole left Deevee in the care of Luke's droids, C-3PO and R2-D2. When they reached the cockpit a moment later, the *Falcon* was flying five kilometers over D'vouran. Leia vacated the copilot's chair so Chewbacca could take over.

Solo glanced down at the churning surface of the planet. "Something strange is happening down there. You're pretty lucky we stopped by."

"Luck had nothing to do with it," Leia said. "Luke suggested we swing back this way and see how you were doing. That's when we saw all four of you on the skimboard."

Hoole spoke quickly. "You must get us out of here as fast as you can."

"No problem," Han Solo drawled. "Whatever's going on down there, you're safe in the *Falcon*."

Han pointed his ship toward outer space, then leaned back and listened as Hoole hastily explained what they had discovered about D'vouran.

Han looked skeptical. "Look, something's obviously churning things up down there. But a living planet? Gotta be a mistake of some kind. We'll sort it out once we're in hyperspace. Chewie, get ready to cut out the sublights."

Chewbacca checked his instruments, then growled.

"What do you mean we're still within D'vouran's gravity?" Solo muttered. "We've been going full thrusters for four minutes. We should be halfway outta this star system by now."

He double-checked the readings. The cocky grin left his face. "I've got a bad feeling about this."

"What is it, Han?" Leia asked.

Solo turned the *Falcon* so that they could just make out D'vouran through the viewport. "I don't think we've gotten away yet."

"What do you mean?" Tash felt her heart sink.

"D'vouran is following us."

CHAPTER

"That's crazy!" Leia said. "Planets don't move."

"Well this one is. And it's getting closer!"

Tash's voice dropped to a horrified whisper. "Didn't you say when you came here, you arrived twenty minutes early?"

"That's right," Luke recalled.

"And we were early, too," Hoole added. He looked out at the planet. At this distance, the writhing ground could not be seen. D'vouran looked calm and beautiful. He muttered, "It does move."

"Can you get into hyperspace, Han?" Luke asked. "We'll be safe there."

"No can do, kid. Not while we're inside the planet's gravity field. And I don't think it plans on letting us out. Chewie, lock in the auxiliary power!"

As Zak, Tash, and the others watched, pilot and co-pilot labored over their controls, pouring every ounce of the *Falcon*'s power into its engines. But when Tash checked the viewport again, D'vouran looked bigger and closer.

"Come on, Han," Leia urged. "You always said this ship was the fastest thing in space."

Sweat poured down Han Solo's brow. "Yeah, well, I never had to race a planet before. Chewie, draw all power from the shields!" The Wookiee growled. "Did that, huh? How about the gun turrets?" Chewbacca snarled. "All right, all right! Just checking."

D'vouran was now close enough to fill the viewport.

Han sat back in his chair. For a split second he looked like he'd been beaten. Then he straightened up. "All right, let's turn the tables on this thing. Gravity's our problem, right? Let's just make it our friend."

He whipped the *Falcon* around hard, throwing everyone off balance. When they recovered, the ship was heading back toward the planet. Chewbacca howled.

"Han, what are you doing!" Luke cried. "You're heading straight for it!"

"Hold on!" the pilot shouted.

Pulled by the planet's gravity and pushed by its own engines, the *Falcon* picked up enormous speed and plunged toward D'vouran. At the last possible moment, Han veered away. Keeping just within gravity's reach, he gunned his engines and scraped along the planet's

135

atmosphere. The belly of his ship left a trail of flames in the air as the freighter looped around the monstrous planet.

The effect was like a slingshot. The vessel whipped around the far side of the planet, and Han broke orbit. Driven by its increased momentum, the *Falcon* was flung out into space, far ahead of D'vouran.

Chewbacca barked a comment. "Gravitational force is dropping!" Han translated.

"You did it!" Leia cried. "We're in open space!"

Freed of D'vouran's gravity, the *Falcon* picked up even more speed.

He turned to his passengers nonchalantly. "The slingshot gimmick. Oldest trick in the manual."

Zak and Tash looked at each other and grinned. Uncle Hoole had not taken his eyes off the planet. "Look," he said.

"I don't believe it," Tash whispered. Even with everything she had seen, she found it hard to grasp what was happening.

The planet D'vouran was squirming. It wriggled and trembled as though trying to change its shape. Bright flashes of light that looked like volcanic eruptions appeared on its surface. The planet bulged outward, becoming a horribly misshapen mass. Then it collapsed in on itself, churning and swirling into a smaller and smaller lump of writhing matter in space. With a final shudder, D'vouran vanished altogether.

"I don't believe it," Zak said.

"Is it gone?" Tash asked.

"It seems to have . . . devoured itself," Hoole said. "Most remarkable."

"Yeah, well we're not sticking around to admire it," said Han. "Chewie, get ready to make the jump. Now!"

The pilot grabbed a large lever and pulled down hard. Zak and Tash were thrown backward as the *Falcon* ripped through the fabric of realspace.

EPILOGUE

In the *Falcon*'s common area, Tash sat across from Uncle Hoole.

"I thought I had been left alone," Tash said. "I thought everyone had been killed. Like my parents."

There was the slightest crack in Hoole's usually grim expression. "I'm sorry, Tash. While you were gone, I saw my chance to spy on the Enzeen. So I became one of them."

"But why did you wait so long to help us?" she demanded. "We could have been killed."

The Shi'ido explained, "I needed to know what was going on. I couldn't find out until Chood spoke to you. I helped you as soon as I could."

"What did you find out?" Princess Leia asked. "What was that thing?"

Hoole said, "I didn't find out much more than Tash did. But my best guess would be this: D'vouran was some kind of scientific experiment that went wrong. The Empire is always experimenting with mutations and biological weapons. They lost control of this one. The pendant was some kind of protective shield. The technology in that small device must have been amazing. I wish I'd been able to study it."

"Well, it couldn't have worked too well," Zak pointed out. "The scientists were all gone. They must have been eaten."

"Were they?" Hoole wondered. "It's just as likely that the creators simply abandoned their project and left it to fend for itself. They may still be out there somewhere."

Tash remembered Chood's evil grin. "And the Enzeen?"

"Parasites, just as you and Deevee guessed. They fed off of D'vouran, and D'vouran allowed them to survive as long as they attracted more food."

"How did they get there?" Zak wondered.

"Maybe they crash-landed like Bebo," Tash suggested, "but the planet didn't like the taste of them."

"Perhaps," Hoole mused. "But I fear the worst. I think whoever is responsible for creating D'vouran also created the Enzeen to watch over and feed the planet. Someone is using science to create mutants."

Luke Skywalker asked the question on everyone's mind. "But whoever is behind these experiments— what are they trying to do?"

"I can't be sure," Hoole replied. "But I intend to find them."

Yet again, Tash remembered Smada's words, and she wondered why Hoole wanted to find these mysterious scientists—to catch them, or join them? She decided to watch him closely.

Aloud, she said gratefully, "Well, whoever it was, at least his experiment is over. D'vouran is gone, and it will never bother anyone again."

Light-years away, in the far reaches of the Outer Rim, in an area of space ignored by both the Empire and the Rebel Alliance, a commuter starship chugged through hyperspace, carrying miners from an asteroid field back to their home planet.

To the pilot's surprise, his passenger ship suddenly dropped out of hyperspace with a jolt. The pilot checked his instruments, and once he was sure his ship was undamaged, he realized that his vessel had fallen into orbit around a beautiful blue-green planet.

"That's odd," he muttered. "I've never seen that on the charts before . . ."

Hoole, Tash, and Zak continue their journeys to the darkest reaches of the galaxy in *City of the Dead*, the next book in the Star Wars: Galaxy of Fear series. For a sneak preview of this book, turn the page!

An excerpt from Star Wars: Galaxy of Fear #2,
City of the Dead:

"Ridiculous."

That was all Boba Fett said in response to Pylum's declaration.

The other Necropolitans didn't seem to believe Pylum either. A few of them even hooted and jeered at the Master of Cerements, despite the overbearing presence of the bounty hunter. But Pylum was undaunted. "You'll see," he said, sweeping his fiery gaze across the crowd in the hostel. "The dead are angry, and they will have their revenge."

The armored bounty hunter waited an extra moment, but no one volunteered any information about Dr. Evazan. Hidden behind his helmet, it was impossible to tell if he was angry, frustrated, or unconcerned. When no one answered his demand, he turned and stalked out of the hostel.

"So that was Boba Fett," Zak breathed. "Prime."

Hoole excused himself to begin his search for their new ship.

"I will return shortly," he said. "Do not leave the hostel grounds." Then, mysterious as always, the Shi'ido slipped out the door.

Zak and Tash spent the rest of the evening at the hostel with their new friend, Kairn. He and Zak took to each other immediately—they had the same sense of mischief and humor. Kairn, it turned out, liked to skimboard as much as Zak did, and they took turns on the hoverboard that Zak kept with him.

Kairn even joined them for dinner at the hostel. When the food was served, the young Necropolitan scooped some of his dinner into a small bowl and put it off to the side without eating it.

"Saving some for later?" Zak joked. He had wolfed down his own food and was about to ask for seconds.

Kairn laughed. "No. It's another old custom. We set aside a portion of every meal in honor of the dead. For most of us, it's more of a tradition now than anything we really believe."

While they ate, Kairn told them more stories about Necropolis and its dark past.

"Lots of legends have built up around the Curse of Sycorax over the centuries. Pylum says that if you visit the graveyard at midnight, you can ask the witch to bring your loved ones back." Kairn chuckled. "Everyone laughs at those stories in the daytime, but I know a few people who more than half believe it, and some who've even tried it."

"Does it only work on buried people?" Zak asked. Beside him, Tash raised an eyebrow, but Zak ignored her and went on. "I mean, does the legend only work on bodies, or could it work on someone who was . . . disintegrated?"

"I don't know. But Pylum says the power of the curse knows no boundaries."

Pylum suddenly loomed over them. His eyes were

filled with eager light. "Our ancestors were fools not to believe in the power of Sycorax. We must believe in the curse of the dead if we are to avoid their mistakes." Pylum glared at them for so long that Zak started to become uncomfortable. Then, without a word, the Master of Cerements turned away.

Tash whispered, "He certainly believes what he's saying, doesn't he?"

Kairn smiled nervously. "He's a fanatic. That's why they made him Master of Cerements."

After dinner, Kairn said he had to get home, but he gave Zak a quick wink and whispered, "Some friends and I have got something fun planned for later. I'll see if I can include you."

Zak grinned. He was beginning to like Kairn.

"So what do you think?" Zak asked Tash after Kairn had gone.

"Think about what?" she replied.

"About these Necropolitans and their beliefs. You know, that the dead come back."

Tash put down her datapad. "Are you kidding? Zak, that's just a legend. Even the Necropolitans don't believe it. Don't tell me you do."

Zak looked down at his shoes. "Um, of course not. But wouldn't it be prime if people really did come back? I mean, if you could see the people you really loved again—"

"Zak." Tash made her voice as gentle as she could manage. When their parents had died, she'd been devastated, and tried to hide herself away in her room. Zak had pulled her out of her misery. Now, she wondered if *he* was finally feeling their loss as much as she had.

"Zak, I miss mom and dad as much as you do. But you can't think that just because of an old superstition, they might actually come back. I know it's hard to think about, but they're gone."

"How do we know?" Zak retorted. Tash's good sense could be really frustrating. "We weren't there. I didn't tell you my whole dream last night," he confessed. "When I saw—when I saw mom, she also asked me something. She asked, 'Why did you leave us behind?' Tash, it was like we abandoned them!"

"Stop it, Zak! We didn't abandon them. They were killed by the Empire. The whole planet was. And as much we hate it, we have to admit it. Mom and Dad are gone. They're not coming back."

But they did come back. That night. As soon as Zak drifted off to sleep.

Zak found himself in his bed in his room on Alderaan again. He turned his head, and looking out the window he saw the darkness of space, dotted with stars.

Tap. Tap. Tap.

He heard the sound of someone rapping at the wall.

Zak tried to sit up, but couldn't. A great weight pressed down on his chest, pinning him in place.

Tap. Tap. Tap.

A pale figure floated into the window's view. It was his mother again. Behind her, another figure floated: his father, his short hair bobbing in the vacuum of space. Their dead skin hung from their lifeless bones, but their mouths moved in a slow, haunting drawl:

"Zak, why did you leave us behind?"

"I didn't," he said hoarsely, "I thought you were dead!"

"You left us behind!"

Tap! Tap!

Their arms banged against the window pane until it shattered inward with a crash.

The two ghostly images floated through the opening. Zak struggled to rise, but he was paralyzed. As they approached, Zak's nostrils filled with the smell of slowly decaying flesh. The corpses' skin was wrinkled and cracked from exposure to the icy cold of space. Their eyes were no more than black holes in their skulls.

"Mom," he whispered. "Dad. I'm sorry . . ."

"Come with us, Zak," his father moaned. "Zak, come with us." The horrible image of his father bent close to him, whispering, "Come with us!"

Zak woke with a start. The image of his dead parents vanished. "It was a dream," he said quickly to himself. It was only a dream.

Crash! Zak almost screamed as something banged against his window again.

———

Zak waited. There were no more crashes.

He finally took a deep breath, and trying to be brave, went over to the transparisteel window and peeked out. There were no monsters or zombies outside. Instead, Zak saw Kairn and a group of boys getting ready to hurl some more stones at his window.

Finally letting his breath out, Zak pressed a button and the automatic window unsealed, letting in the cool night air. He leaned out.

Kairn waved and laughed. "Sorry about that. I figured you'd want to come along with us."

"Where?" Zak asked.

"Some friends and I are having a little midnight adventure. Into the graveyard," Kairn said mischievously. "Care to join us? Unless, of course, you're too *scared*?"

Zak couldn't resist a taunt like that. "I'm right behind you."

Throwing on some clothes, Zak tiptoed out of his room. Zak went quietly past the rooms of Tash and Uncle Hoole. At the end of the hall, he froze. There was Deevee, sitting in a chair at the top of the stairs.

"The bionic babysitter," Zak muttered. "Looks like this will be one short trip."

But as he crept closer, Zak realized that Deevee had shut himself down for the night. He would not power up unless someone came in range of his sensor field, activating his systems. The field only reached a half meter out from the droid's metal body, but Zak still had no desire to get caught by the sarcastic droid while trying to sneak out.

Better not risk it, he told himself. There was always the window.

Zak was two levels up from the ground, but the building was covered in elaborate, ghoulish carvings. He started down, using the heads, and arms, and claws of the carved monsters like a weird ladder. He stuck his hand into the roaring jaw of a six-legged beast and quietly called down to Kairn, "What are these carvings?"

"Just more legends," Kairn said, holding out his arms ready to catch Zak. "The statues are supposed to frighten away evil spirits. If you ask me, they make better handholds."

On the ground, Kairn introduced Zak to a small group of Necropolitans, all about his age.

"So this is the offworlder that shoved you, huh?" one of them said to Kairn. "He doesn't look so brave to me."

"Yeah," teased another. "I bet he's an easy scare."

Zak was annoyed. "Are you joking? After the last planet I was on, this place is like a vacation."

"That's just what we wanted to hear!" said Kairn. He lowered his voice to a conspiratorial whisper. "But before you can join our group, there's a little test you have to pass."

"Yeah, we're particular about who joins our group," said another.

"Most people in Necropolis say they don't believe

the old legends, but they're still scared of their own shadows," Kairn continued. "At the landing bay you proved you were a little brave, but we need to make sure."

Zak scowled. "What kind of test?"

"Come on, we'll show you."

Kairn led the group of Necropolitan boys down the winding streets of the dark city. Zak followed eagerly. He was on a new planet, walking through a gloomy alien city in the middle of the night with a group of boys he had only just met, but he felt at home for the first time in months.

He had lost all his friends when Alderaan was destroyed. Uncle Hoole hardly talked to him. Deevee was all right but he wasn't the kind of friend who would help you climb out of your bedroom window in the middle of the night. Tash, Zak had to admit, could be a good friend sometimes, but she was his *sister*, so in his book it didn't really count.

But these boys, especially Kairn, reminded Zak of his own group back on Alderaan. They had never caused any real trouble, of course, but they had their share of fun. Once, Zak and some of his school friends had snuck into the teacher's washroom at their school and replaced the mirror with a hologram screen programmed to reflect anyone's image exactly—only twenty kilos heavier. Snack sales at the instructors' cantina had plummeted until the prank was discovered.

Now, for the first time in half a year, Zak felt like he

had a chance to run with his own crowd. He decided instantly that he was going to make the most of it. By the time they reached their destination, Zak was laughing and joking with Kairn like they were old friends.

"This is it," Kairn said as they stopped in front of a huge, black wrought-iron gate.

Zak couldn't see beyond it the thick mist of Necropolis. "What is it?"

One of the other boys said ominously, "It's the Cemetery."

"The boneyard," Kairn added.

"Sacred ground!" said another in his best imitation of Pylum. They all laughed.

But Zak was too awestruck to smile. The Cemetery was enormous. Beyond the black gates, row upon row of graves stretched on forever into the darkness.

"It's huge," he whispered.

"That's the true Necropolis," Kairn said. "The city of the dead."

"It's the most popular place in the city," one of the others joked morbidly. "Everyone goes there. Eventually."

Zak asked, "You mean everyone's buried here? It must be crowded."

"I suppose, but so far no one's complained," Kairn said, laughing. "Here's the challenge. You have to go into the graveyard in the dead of night, and stand on a grave in the middle of the cemetery."

"Go in there?" Zak said hoarsely. He peered through

the gate, imagining the rows of dead stacked just below the ground.

"Sure," Kairn said. "What have you got to lose?"

"His nerve," one of the others teased.

Zak considered. "If I accepted, what else would I have to do?"

Kairn grinned. "Not much. Just get to the middle of the cemetery and back."

Zak peered through the iron gates. The mist made it hard to see. Through the drifting clouds of gray fog he could just barely make out the first line of headstones in the darkness.

"Maybe he's too scared after all," said one of the boys.

"I'm not scared," Zak insisted.

The mist is so thick, he told himself, *that they'll hardly be able to see me ten meters beyond the gate. How will they know how far I've gone?*

"It's a bet," he said with a gleam in his eye.

"Good." Kairn said. "All you have to do is go in and follow any path. They all lead to the center of the graveyard, where you'll see a large tomb. That's the Crypt of the Ancients. According to legend, that's where they buried Sycorax and her son. Pick any of the graves around the Crypt, stand right on top of it, and then come back."

The wrought iron gate was unsealed. Kairn pulled and the gate opened with a mournful squeal. Zak was about to step in, when his new friend stopped him.

"Oh, I almost forgot," Kairn said with a grin. "You'll need this."

He handed Zak a small dagger.

"What for?"

"You have to stick it in the ground in the middle of a grave near the Crypt of the Ancients. Tomorrow morning we'll go and see if it's there. For proof."

So much for his plan. Zak shivered.

"He looks scared!" someone teased.

"Just cold," Zak lied.

"Here, take this." Kairn gave Zak this thick cloak. "And you'll need this, too." He handed Zak a tiny glowrod to use for light.

Zak wrapped the heavy cloak around his shoulders and took a step into the graveyard, holding the glowrod in front of him. Its light barely penetrated the rolling mist. Row after row of tombstones vanished into the darkness before him. He took a few more steps. The headstones looked like a miniature city. A city of the dead.

"Good luck!" Kairn whispered behind him. "Oh, and watch out for the boneworms."

"Boneworms?" Zak hissed. "What are boneworms?"

"Nothing, really," Kairn chuckled. "Just wriggling creatures that come out of the ground. They'll suck the marrow from your bones if you stay still long enough!"

The iron gate slammed shut behind Zak.

ABOUT THE AUTHOR

John Whitman has written several interactive adventures for *Where in the World Is Carmen Sandiego?*, as well as many Star Wars stories for audio and print. He is an executive editor for Time Warner Audiobooks and lives in Los Angeles.